FICTION HOUSE PRESS
PRESENTS

THRILLING DETECTIVE

October 1948
Vol. LXII, No. 3

This reprint edition is a facsimile of the original pulp magazine. Variations in printing and quality can be attributed to the original magazine which was printed on rough woodpulp paper.

ISBN 978-1-64720-116-6

www.FictionHousePress.com
fictionhousepress@gmail.com

IF you're that man, here's something that will interest you.

Not a magic formula—not a get-rich-quick scheme—but something more substantial, more practical.

Of course, you need something more than just the desire to be an accountant. You've got to pay the price—be willing to study earnestly, thoroughly.

Still, wouldn't it be worth your while to sacrifice some of your leisure in favor of interesting home study—over a comparatively brief period in your life? Always provided that the rewards were good—a salary of $3,000 to $10,000?

An accountant's duties are interesting, varied and of real worth to his employers. He has *standing!*

Do you feel that such things aren't for you? Well, don't be too sure. Very possibly they *can* be!

Why not, like so many before you, investigate LaSalle's modern Problem Method of training for an accountancy position?

Just suppose you were permitted to work in a large accounting house under the personal supervision of an expert accountant. Suppose, with his aid, you studied accounting principles and solved problems day by day—easy ones at first—then the more difficult ones. If you could do this—and if you could turn to him for advice as the problems became complex—soon you'd master them all.

That's the training you follow in principle under the LaSalle Problem Method.

You cover accountancy from the basic Principles right up through Accountancy Systems and Income Tax Procedure. Then you add C. P. A. Training and prepare for the C. P. A. examinations.

As you go along, you absorb the principles of Auditing, Cost Accounting, Business Law, Statistical Control, Organization, Management and Finance.

Your progress is as speedy as you care to make it—depending on your own eagerness to learn and the time you spend in study.

Will recognition come? The only answer, as you know, is that success *does* come to the man who is really *trained.* It's possible your employers will notice your improvement in a very few weeks or months. Indeed, many LaSalle graduates have paid for their training—with increased earnings—before they have completed it! For accountants, who are trained in organization and management, are the executives of the future.

Write For This Free Book

For your own good, don't put off investigation of *all* the facts. Write for our free 48-page book, "Accountancy, The Profession That Pays." It'll prove that accountancy offers brilliant futures to those who aren't afraid of serious home study. Send us the coupon *now.*

Over 2600 Certified Public Accountants among LaSalle alumni

LASALLE EXTENSION UNIVERSITY

A CORRESPONDENCE INSTITUTION

417 South Dearborn Street, Dept. 10329-H Chicago 5, Illinois

I want to be an accountant. Send me, without cost or obligation, the 48-page book, "Accountancy, The Profession That Pays," and full information about your accountancy training program.

Name..

Address.. *City*..............................

Position.. *Age*..............................

THRILLING DETECTIVE

Vol. LXII, No. 3 A THRILLING PUBLICATION OCTOBER, 1948

Published every other month by Standard Magazines, Inc., 10 East 40th Street, New York 16, N. Y. N. L. Pines, President. Subscription (12 issues), $1.80; single copies, $.15. Foreign and Canadian postage extra. Re-entered as second-class matter, July 27, 1945, at the Post Office at New York, N. Y., under Act of March 3, 1879.

PRINTED IN THE U. S. A.

LEARN RADIO

BY PRACTICING IN SPARE TIME

As part of my Course, I send you the speaker, tubes, chassis, transformer, loop antenna, EVERYTHING you need to build this modern, powerful Radio Receiver! In addition I send you parts to build other real Radio circuits, some of which are pictured below. You use material to get practical Radio experience and make EXTRA money fixing neighbors' Radios in spare time.

I SEND YOU BIG KITS OF PARTS

You Build and Experiment With this MODERN RADIO

AND MANY OTHER CIRCUITS

J. E. SMITH, President
National Radio Institute

Want a good-pay job in the fast-growing Radio Industry—or your own Radio Shop? Mail coupon for Actual Lesson and 64-page book, "How to Be a Success in Radio-Television-Electronics." Both FREE! See how I train you at home—how you get practical Radio experience building, testing Radio circuits with BIG KITS OF PARTS I send.

Make EXTRA Money While Learning

The day you enroll I send EXTRA money manuals, show you how to make EXTRA money fixing neighbors' Radios in spare time. It's probably easier than ever to start now, because Radio Repair Business is booming. Trained Radio Technicians find profitable opportunities in Police, Aviation, Broadcasting, Marine Radio, Public Address work. Think of even greater opportunities as demand for Television, FM, Electronic Devices keeps growing!

SEE What NRI Can Do For You!

Mail Coupon for FREE Lesson and 64-page book. Read details about my Course, letters from men I trained about what they now earn. See how quickly, easily you can get started. No obligation! Mail Coupon in envelope or paste on penny postal. Send NOW! J. E. SMITH, Pres., Dept. 8K09, National Radio Inst., Pioneer Home Study Radio School, Washington 9, D. C.

I TRAINED THESE MEN

"AM NOW GETTING $60 a week and overtime as Radio Serviceman for The Adams Appliance Co."—W. A. ANGEL, Blythesville, Arkansas.

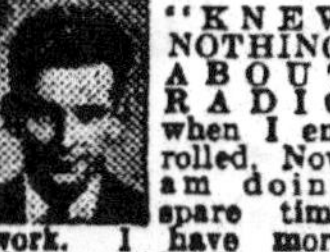

"KNEW NOTHING ABOUT RADIO when I enrolled. Now am doing spare time work. I have more than paid for my Course and about $200 worth of equipment."—RAYMOND HOLTCAMP, Vandalia, Ill.

VETERANS

You can get this training under G. I. Bill. Mail Coupon.

My Course Includes Training in
TELEVISION • ELECTRONICS
FREQUENCY MODULATION

Good for Both-FREE

MR. J. E. SMITH, President, Dept. 8K09
NATIONAL RADIO INSTITUTE, Washington 9, D. C.

Mail me FREE Sample Lesson and 64-page book. (No salesman will call. Please write plainly.)

Age______

Name______

Address______

City______ Zone____ State____

☐ Check if Veteran

The breaking waves dashed high,
On a stern and rock-bound coast.

THESE famous words of the Nineteenth Century poetess, Felicia D. Hemans, come to mind as a fitting introduction for our complete novel in the forthcoming issue of THRILLING DETECTIVE magazine—HAUNT ME NO MORE, by Edward Ronns.

It is in and around the beach at Bar Haven—or in the luxurious home of the Porter family, traditionally austere and straight-laced—but mostly aboard the schooner *Five Kings,* somewhere between Cape Cod and the Grand Banks, that the action of this stirring story takes place. A yarn shrouded in mystery as deep and gray as the murky fog. A yarn with the tang of exciting adventure, as keen as the salty spray of the windswept sea.

The body of Danny Porter has been washed ashore. The head has been bashed in and he has been shot. It is quite palpably murder.

Of course, the body isn't too easy to identify. It has been in the water for at least two weeks. It *must* be Danny, on account of the ring. Yet . . . it could be David.

Two of a Kind

You see, Danny and David Porter are identical twins. Very few people can tell them apart—although Linda Hayes always says she can. She does not know why—yet everybody else knows that Linda loves David, even though she is not aware of it herself.

When they find the body, Linda Hayes feels that David should be notified, even though David is said to be at sea on board the fishing schooner *Five Kings.* They can at least leave word for him when he puts in at Boston. But Amos Stillmeadow doesn't want David notified. Amos is Linda's employer and also David's uncle.

There is another voice raised in protest against the call. It is a softer, sweeter and more seductive voice, but it is insistent nonetheless. It is the voice of beautiful and voluptuous Janet Porter, who is Danny Porter's wife—and now his widow, perchance.

A Struggle for Life

The scene shifts to the schooner *Five Kings* and David Porter is aboard her, supervising the fishing. It is then that a red-bearded, tremendous hulk of a man, Captain Clint Fowler, tells David that the schooner he commands is due to return to Boston. David Porter argues that the fish are running now and it would be senseless to go back. He points out that he is the owner of the vessel, in order to combat the ancient Law of the Sea that the captain is in supreme command.

The next thing David knows he is struggling for life itself, in the mighty bosom of the Atlantic. He does not know if someone hit him or there was a collision or what. Barely conscious, he manages to reach the deck of the schooner, where, almost drowned and retching, he collapses again.

When he finally comes into full possession of his faculties, he is aboard the schooner right enough, but the vessel is tied up to her wharf in Boston Harbor. David knows, by now, that in order to get off the boat he will have to fight.

Fight he does, friends, in spite of his weakened condition—hand-to-hand, with a man a good thirty pounds heavier than he is.

(Continued on page 8)

HEADQUARTERS

(Continued from page 6)

But he makes it, and reaches a Boston hotel, where Linda brings him clothes. He returns safely to Bar Haven to face his uncle and his brother's wife—or whose wife?

Puzzling Questions

Why had Janet suddenly decided to marry Danny when everybody knew she loved David? Why did David, brilliant concert pianist that he was, decide to cancel his tour when he heard the news of his brother's marriage? Also, how did Linda, doing a little detective work on her own hook, find that record of Janet's marriage? There, in bold handwriting, the name of the groom was—David Porter!

These questions are answered, and the mystery of the twins unraveled, in HAUNT ME NO MORE, by Edward Ronns—as gripping a mystery as we have ever presented! A mystery in which you'll find something new and refreshing in the way of clever detective work. Look forward to it!

Crime in the Ring

Another grand yarn next issue is WITH DEATH IN HIS CORNER, by Louis L'Amour. This is an action-packed novelet of that most maligned game, the fight racket. Lots of people have written about it, but few understand the boxing game as well as our author, Mr. L'Amour, who has previously given us several vivid pictures of that former pugilist, now private detective—the indomitable Kip Morgan.

Kip is of the opinion that there is something suspicious about the disappearance of his old pal along Cauliflower Row, one Rocky Garzo. True—Garzo was a bit punchy now and didn't seem to know what it was all about. Morgan knew however, that Garzo had laid aside any connection with the seamy end of the business and was trying—as much as he could—to go straight. That is why he'd taken a job in the Crystal Palace, a sort of a down-at-the-heels saloon and night club.

When Morgan enters this shoddy emporium of tinsel, they take him for a wolf on his night to howl—especially that dame at the table with the bald-headed fellow. To quote our author, the "new look didn't

(Continued on page 10)

HEADQUARTERS

(Continued from page 8)

keep the boys from giving her the old look—not with the set of fixtures she had!"

Hotter Than a Firecracker

But when Morgan starts inquiring about Rocky Garzo, he gets large chunks of the old brush-off. Headwaiters, waiters—bouncers—they never heard of him. But Morgan knows better. Didn't that letter from the ex-pug, even now, burn a hole in his pocket? Garzo isn't in the habit of writing that he's in trouble. As a matter of fact, Rocky Garzo isn't in the habit of writing at all.

Morgan knows well enough that Garzo is a kid who never had a thing until he got into the money in the fight game, and he likes good food, flashy women and clothes. His money just sort of dribbles away and the easy life is beginning to tell on him.

Thinking back upon all this, Morgan is amazed to hear the soft and cultured voice of the girl at the next table. She speaks, yet never even turns her head:

"You better take it out of here. The friend you're looking for is hotter than a firecracker and I don't mean with the law. If you don't lay off—you'll find your number's up and these boys play rough—even for you, Kip Morgan!"

The slick chick offers to meet the detective at the Silver Plate in half an hour. Morgan gets further information from one Pete Farber, who is bouncer there. Farber has good reason to remember Kip—although the last time they mixed, Farber's eyes were so puffed from the beating he took, that he couldn't see *anybody*.

The Big Wheel

Morgan begins now, to trace behind everything, the fine hand of one Ben Altman, former light-heavyweight, who has moved in as the Big Wheel in the racing wires and reefer racket. So when Kip enters that dingy rooming-house and sees, lying on the soiled bed, the body of Rocky Garzo, a knife in his back, he knows he has met a subtle foe-man, all too worthy of his steel.

Then the gun with the silencer on it coughs and the ping of the bullet whistles through the air—

And that's all you're going to get of that

(Continued on page 111)

THINGS BROKE RIGHT FOR PAT WHEN...

QUIZ
PARIS!
RIGHT FOR $500! NOW GO DOWNSTAIRS TO ROE'S STORE FOR ANOTHER PRIZE!
TIRED AND DISHEARTENED AFTER A LONG DAY OF ATTEMPTING TO SELL HIS FIRST PLAY, YOUNG PAT MARTIN HAD JUST DROPPED IN TO WATCH A RADIO QUIZ SHOW. BUT THEN...

MINUTES LATER
PLEASE...IT WAS AN ACCIDENT. I'M PENNILESS. I'VE BEEN SICK AND OUT OF WORK
YOU BROKE IT! PAY ME TEN DOLLARS OR I'LL CALL A COP!
I'LL HELP HER OUT!

YOU MEAN...?
YES, IT WAS ALL A PUT-UP JOB TO TEST YOUR CHARITY. NOW LET'S GET BACK TO THE STUDIO, YOU'RE NOT THROUGH YET!

WE HAVE DINNER CLOTHES FOR YOU BACKSTAGE. AFTER YOU CHANGE, TAKE THE LADY OUT AND DO THE TOWN ON US
WOW!

A RAZOR? RIGHT HERE, SIR

WHAT A SLICK-SHAVING BLADE! MY FACE FEELS GREAT!
IT LOOKS GREAT, TOO. THIN GILLETTES ARE PLENTY KEEN

TELL OUR AUDIENCE YOUR PLANS, PAT
WELL, DINNER, THEN A GOOD SHOW AND THEN A NIGHT CLUB, IF THE LADY'S WILLING
WHAT A CHANGE! HE'S HANDSOME!

IF MY BROTHER LIKES YOUR PLAY, IT'S AS GOOD AS SOLD. HE'S THE BEST AGENT IN TOWN
GREAT! THEN I'LL CALL FOR YOU TOMORROW AT THE STUDIO
SHE'S TERRIFIC!
AFTER THE SHOW

YOU ALWAYS GET SMOOTH, PLEASANT SHAVES THAT MAKE YOU LOOK AND FEEL SWELL WITH THIN GILLETTES...THE KEENEST, LONGEST-LASTING BLADES IN THE LOW-PRICE FIELD. ALSO YOU AVOID THE SCRAPE AND IRRITATION OF MISFIT BLADES WHEN YOU USE THIN GILLETTES IN YOUR GILLETTE RAZOR. THEY ARE PRECISION-MADE TO FIT EXACTLY. ENJOY TRUE SHAVING COMFORT WITH THIN GILLETTES
THIN Gillette BLADES
4-10¢
10-25¢
New ten-blade package has compartment for used blades.

When Private Detective Walt Bonner arrived at the racetracks, he was there to help a pretty night club owner make a killing—but he didn't expect the type of "killing" that was going on!

DON'T *tell anyone*

CHAPTER I

Easy Assignment

I WAS within a few steps of the entrance of the Heathers Hotel when the little man came out.

I stopped for a moment, and watched him. I recalled vaguely seeing him at the McBains party the night before. Arthur Detman, his name was. He had been quiet at the party and had left early.

A strange little man. He was very neat, in a blue black suit; very precise, very courteous. He was not over five feet tall, with narrow shoulders and an

a novelet by J. LANE LINKLATER

impressive-looking paunch. He wasn't old, I thought; probably not over forty, yet his face seemed shriveled.

Arthur Detman stepped briskly into a taxi and was driven rapidly away.

I felt a queer sense of eagerness as I pushed through into the large lush lobby. Maybe the girl's voice had had something to do with that. I didn't think much about it, having inherited a headache from the party.

I felt grateful for the soft lights, as I moved through the acres of palms toward the far southwest corner of the lobby, which was where she had told me to go.

"And," she had added, "don't tell anyone you are going there."

I spotted her instantly, a smooth slim article reclining in a big leather chair, smoking a cigarette. I was standing over her almost before I realized it—and before she realized it. Her head was tilted back, and her upturned face showed fine straight features, the blue-gray eyes lively, and the full lips warm.

"Good morning, Miss Savoy," I said. "Cocktail parties don't appear to leave any scars on you."

She straightened in her chair and glanced up at me swiftly, looking me over.

The one thing she could see in me was length; long legs, long arms, long face.

She smiled. "You look okay yourself, Walt Bonner."

"Except for the face."

"That's okay, too. I like them grim."

I sat down close to her. The spot was screened by a row of potted palms. The windows in front of us looked out on a side street.

"Did you see Arthur Detman?" I said.

She frowned. "Detman?"

"Yes. Funny little guy who was at the party last night. I just saw him leave the hotel."

"Oh, I remember him now. No, I didn't see him. Why?"

"I don't know. You know him well?"

"Oh, no. I've seen him around several places in the last few weeks, now that you mention it. But he always keeps in the background. He has some kind of a little business, I think someone told me. An accountancy office, or something of the kind."

SO I SHUNTED Arthur Detman out of my mind.

"I got a little fuzzy at the party last night," I said. "I seem to remember there was a young lady present—a smash hit for looks—by the name of Reva Savoy. I had never met her before. I didn't have much chance to talk to her, but I spent a lot of time looking at her."

"Kind of you," Reva Savoy said primly.

"Not at all. Then, quite late, this beauty came to me and asked me to call here at eleven o'clock this morning."

"And here you are!"

"Yes. But it's not a good idea—unless it's strictly business."

"Oh. Why not?"

"The obvious folly of a guy who has nothing getting tangled up with a dame who has plenty," I said briskly, and peered at her anxiously. "This *is* business, isn't it?"

"It certainly is." Reva's laugh was only faintly nervous. "So you're broke, Walt?"

"Practically. Before the war, I had a father, and the father had cash aplenty. I came back from distant lands to find that good old Dad had passed on, and somehow he had lost his cash first. So that's why I happened to remark, at the party, that I was figuring on opening a private agency. I haven't even got a license yet, but it appears that you already want to make use of my gifts. Let's get to work."

"I think," Reva said thoughtfully, "I should tell you that I want you for only a short assignment, which will pay you well—if you're lucky. I should also mention that it might be dangerous."

"My head still aches," I said. "Please make it simple."

She snapped open a small, modish brown purse. Her long slender fingers plucked at something inside.

"Hold out your hand," she said.

I did, palm up. Casually, she counted eleven one-hundred-dollar bills into the hand. I looked at the cash. "What do I do with all this wealth?"

"You go out to the track this after-

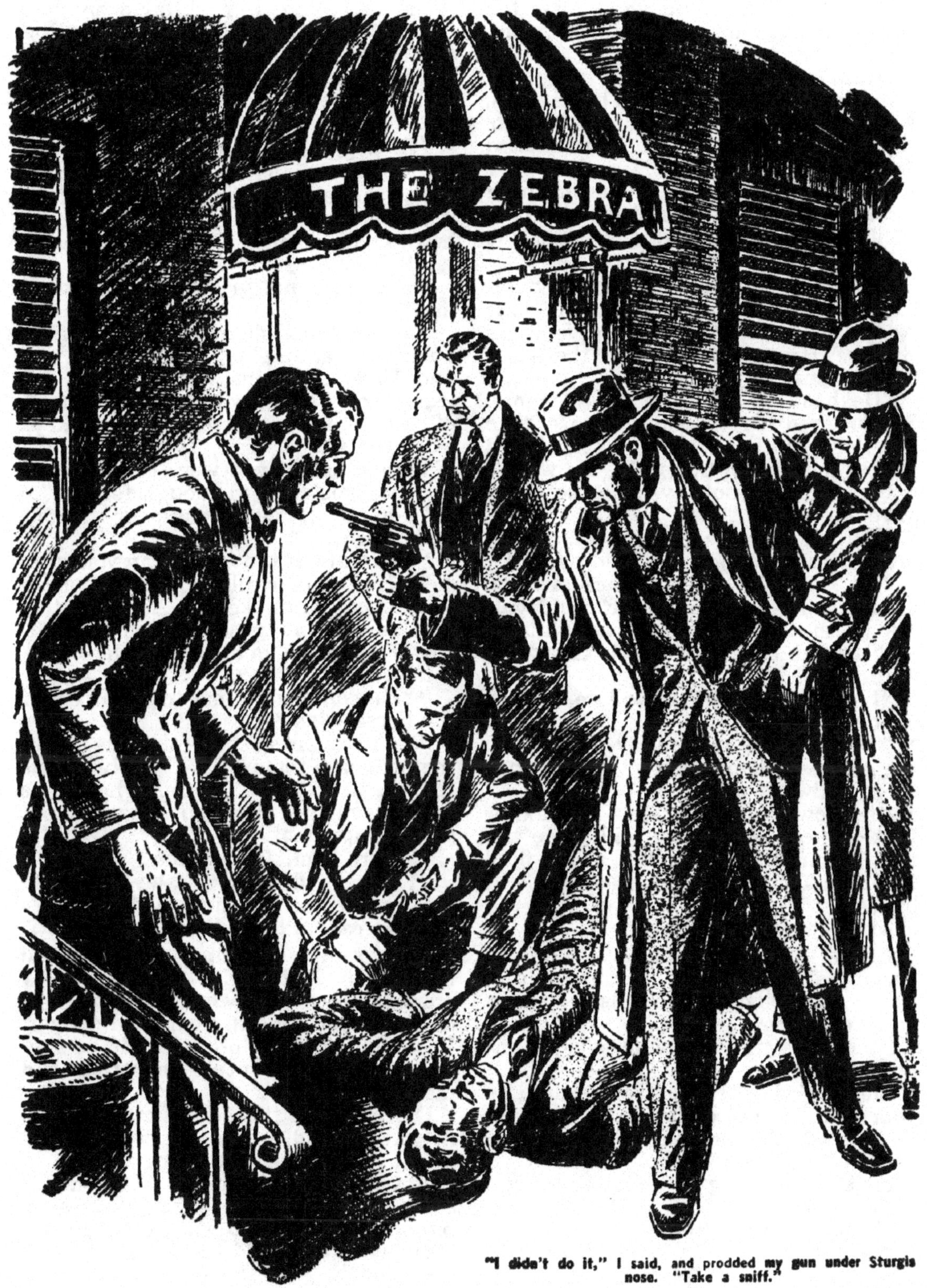

"I didn't do it," I said, and prodded my gun under Sturgis nose. "Take a sniff."

noon," she said. "And you wager the money on a horse named Adams' Atom. This horse is number three in the seventh race." She smiled brightly. "And, since you appear to be curious, Adams' Atom is a small horse with lots of power, owned by a man named Adams."

I had a folded copy of the morning *Times* in my pocket. I unfolded it to the racing page, ran my finger down the tabulated entries for the day.

"This journalistic tout," I said dubiously, "doesn't think much of your Adams' Atom. Doesn't even give him a chance. His comment is that the Atom hasn't shown anything yet."

"He hasn't," conceded Reva calmly. She lowered her pleasant voice. "The few times he's been entered he's finished well at the back of the pack. He wasn't ready anyway—but, even so, he could have done better."

"Tut," I said disapprovingly. "You mean he was deliberately held back?"

"No. But the owner, Jack Adams, used the poorest jockeys he could get. Today, the Atom is ready, and Adams will use the best he can get. Makes a difference."

"I hope you can afford to lose," I said doubtfully.

"That," Reva said tartly, "is beside the point. I know perfectly well that there's always a chance of losing, no matter how good the set-up. I'm taking that chance. The Atom will go to the post a long-shot, probably about fifty to one. That means a thousand will bring me fifty thousand. I can use the extra money."

I eyed the girl skeptically. She was smooth, she was smart, she had nerve. But it was obvious she wasn't telling me everything.

"You gave me a thousand, plus a hundred," I said.

She smiled. "The extra hundred is your fee. If you're playing safe, you'll just pocket the hundred. But if you're what I think you are you'll put it on Adams' Atom along with my thousand."

"To win?"

"Right smack on the nose!"

"Look," I said. "You don't need to hire anyone just to place a bet. Why not handle it yourself?"

She had an answer. "Obviously, it is better for me to have the bet placed at the track, and it so happens I can't go out to the track this afternoon."

"Why not?"

SHE wiggled a finger at me.

"That is distinctly my own business," she said. "It could be a love affair. And the reason I picked you is that I had to have someone I could trust absolutely."

That made me grin. "So you trust me?"

"As much as I do anyone. I inquired about you last night. I understand you and Ernie McBains were pals at college. You went to war together. Ernie, of course, didn't come back." Reva looked a little wistful. "I was very fond of Ernie, and if you were good enough for him, you're good enough for me."

"You mean, good enough for this one assignment."

"Certainly, if that's the way you want it." Her voice chilled. "All you have to do is buy the tickets on Adams' Atom just as close to post time as possible. You'll deliver them to me at eight o'clock this evening."

"You don't want me to cash 'em if the horse wins?"

"No. I can cash them any time before the fifth race tomorrow. Just bring me the tote tickets, win or lose. The tickets will be evidence that you've carried out your assignment."

"Where shall I meet you?"

"I have a flat on Chesley Avenue." She handed me a calling card. "Here's the address. Please be there at eight."

She got up. I got up, too, slowly, and looked down at her. I was certainly puzzled about the whole set-up. She had said there was an element of danger. I couldn't see it. Nothing could be simpler than going out to the track and placing a bet.

Of course, if the horse actually won, fifty thousand bucks in tote tickets might tempt some guy with a gun.

Reva's voice softened. "Thanks for coming, Walt. And watch your step, please. . . . I won't walk through the lobby with you. I'd rather not be seen with you."

"I don't blame you," I said, laughing.

She flushed faintly.

"You know what I mean—just on account of the business. Otherwise, I wouldn't mind."

But she *was* seen with me. Right away. A man came strolling around the row of palms and almost collided with us. He was almost as tall as I, and a few years older. There was a hook-nosed distinction about his face, and a careless arrogance in his bearing.

"So here you are, Reva!" he exclaimed, and I wondered if he was as surprised as he appeared to be. "I've been looking all over for you!"

I was watching Reva. Her control was wonderful. There was just a brief blinking of her eyelashes, then she was smiling serenely.

"Sorry, Sid," she said. "I just happened to run into Walt Bonner here. We met at the McBains last night, you know. You met him, too, didn't you?"

The guy had been at the party and I remembered him.

"Well, yes," he said. And I said "Oh, sure."

We shook hands.

Then I said I was sorry, but I'd have to be going. And I went, wondering what, if anything, Sid Towne knew about all this.

On the way out I stopped at the desk and asked the clerk if Sid Towne was a resident of the hotel. The clerk didn't even have to look it up.

"Mr. Towne is one of our regulars," he said.

"How about Arthur Detman?" I said, happening to think of that queer little man.

"Detman?" said the clerk. He riffled through some cards. "No, sir. No Detman is registered here."

CHAPTER II

SUDDEN POPULARITY

I HAD plenty of time. I could run out to the track in forty minutes. It wasn't quite noon, and the seventh race wasn't scheduled until five o'clock. I walked three blocks and stopped in a small café. Over a plate of beef stew

Slumped in the back of my car, with blood streaking his face, was a little man in a sporty green outfit

I reflected on Sid Towne. I knew nothing about him; only that he appeared to be a man of independent means and had a constant interest in Reva Savoy.

I lingered long over three cups of coffee. It was past one o'clock when I stopped lingering.

My own apartment was over a mile away. I walked it. The apartment was one of six in a three-story building; two on each floor. The building was ancient, the apartment small, the rent low—which was the index to my current resources.

My place was on the second floor. I unlocked the street door, trudged up the narrow stairs. On the landing above I stopped suddenly. I didn't quite know what it was—perhaps a faint noise, although I couldn't place it, wasn't even sure I had heard it.

Just in front of me was the living room door. I opened the door, quietly, and stepped in. The sparsely furnished room was quiet. I stood just inside the door, eyes searching.

There was a closet in the far corner. The closet door was gently swinging.

The threadbare carpet muffled my footsteps as I crossed the room. I stood quietly for a little while, staring at the door.

Then I yanked it open.

A small man in a sporty green suit stood inside, quite motionless. A gun in his hand pointed rigidly at my middle. The gimlet eyes in the ferret face were sharp and bright.

"Come on out and be comfortable," I said.

The fellow's lips worked. He seemed uncertain what to do. "Back up, pal," he said suddenly.

I thought about it a moment, then backed away from the closet. The man came out slowly, warily. I was backstepping slowly. Then I shifted gears and dashed forward. My fist caught him under the chin, lifted him off his feet and sent him crashing back into the closet.

His gun flipped up in the air and landed on a couch.

"Get up," I said.

The man was squirming, whining. He managed to get up.

"Sit down," I said.

He dropped in a chair.

"What's your name?"

He was silent. I stepped up to him, lifted him easily by clutching his shirt in front, shook him.

"What's your name?"

"Johnson."

An obvious lie, of course. I dropped him in the chair, started rummaging through his pockets. He resisted at first, and I slapped him quiet again. In one pocket I found a wallet, with money and papers. I looked at the address on an envelope.

"So you're Chet Martin?"

He shrugged nervously.

"What were you looking for?" I said.

He had nothing to say to that, either.

"You know Reva Savoy?" I said.

He actually talked then. "I could maybe have heard the name some place."

"You also know Sid Towne?"

Chet Martin licked his lips and said nothing.

I glanced at a sheet of notepaper, folded, which I had taken out of the wallet. It was an elegant sheet of excellent quality. The initials engraved on it were: "ST." The only writing on it was in pencil—the address of my apartment.

I chucked the wallet with its contents at Martin. He caught it eagerly and pocketed it.

Obviously, there was no use questioning this rat. The fellow wouldn't tell the truth short of being tortured into it, and I had no stomach for that. Besides, he annoyed me.

"Get out of here," I said.

Chet Martin jumped out of the chair and scurried across the room. I listened to his footsteps pelting down the stairs.

I SAT down and thought about it. I couldn't get anything out of it except that this Chet Martin seemed to be tied up with Sid Towne.

I recalled then that at the party, my mind being momentarily clouded by the fumes of a cocktail, I had told Towne where I lived, and I thought he had made a note of it. Usually, I kept my address secret. For no special reason except that under present conditions I wasn't encouraging visitors.

On a hunch, I reached for the phone. I called the Heathers Hotel and hoped I was right in assuming that Reva was lunching there with Sid Towne. I asked that Miss Savoy be paged.

Luck was with me. In two or three minutes I heard her voice. She seemed a little sorry I had called.

"You know a guy named Chet Martin?" I said bluntly.

"Yes."

"Tell me about him."

"Martin used to work for Jack Adams as a stable man," Reva said. "A few months ago Adams caught him in some dirty work and fired him."

"What's he been doing since?"

"I don't know. I've seen him around. He seems to have money enough to live."

"Maybe he gets the money from Sid Towne," I said.

Reva was silent a moment. Then she said: "I know nothing of that. I think Martin hung around Sid for a while after he was fired, but not lately."

"If Towne isn't paying him money now," I said, "somebody else certainly is."

"I really couldn't say," Reva said frostily.

"Okay. So can you tell me why Chet Martin would visit my apartment—in my absence?"

"I have no idea." Her voice seemed a trifle shaken. "You mean he—"

"I mean I found him in my place."

"What did you do with him?"

"Threw him out."

"But couldn't you make him tell why he was there?"

"No. He would only lie, anyway." I added gruffly, "It seems to me you should tell me more."

"About what?"

"About what goes on."

"Sorry," she said curtly. "You took a job, but if you want to back out, it's all right with me."

"Okay, okay. See you tonight at eight."

Gloomily, I dropped the receiver. Reva had certainly called me on that. She was right, too. I had, after all, taken the assignment with a definite warning.

But I wondered if she was really being smart. Maybe it would have been better for her, as well as for me, if she had given me the complete picture.

And so far as Chet Martin was concerned, I didn't believe he was looking for any one thing in particular in my rooms. I didn't see how he could be. Most likely he was just trying to get a line on me—for somebody else, no doubt.

The discordant ringing of my door bell snapped at me. I hesitated a moment. My address was practically unknown to any of my old friends, and I couldn't understand this sudden popularity.

I went to the landing at the head of the stairs and pressed the button. Below, the door lock clicked, and the door was pushed open.

The man who stepped in was large and portly, and sloppily dressed in banker's gray.

He looked up, saw me, said "Hah!" and plodded up the stairs. Then he was standing on the landing with me. With great dignity in spite of his wheezing, he stared at me out of round, solemn eyes.

"You are Walt Bonner?" he said.

"Sure. Come in and sit down."

He waddled into the living room after me, a walking cane tucked under his arm. He sank cautiously into a scaly armchair and studied me intently.

"I am Amos Dunlop," he said. "I am greatly concerned about Miss Reva Savoy. I understand she has entered into a deal with you."

"It's funny about that," I said warily. "She told me not to tell anyone. How come you know about it?"

DUNLOP waved a fat hand.

"I know nothing of the details, young man. I was talking to her this morning, on the phone. She didn't tell me everything. But I've known her many years—since she was a mere child. I knew her parents intimately. I have a special interest in her."

"Okay. So what's your angle?"

He raised a feeble eyebrow. "Angle? Frankly, I don't want anything. I'm just worried about Reva."

"So you wanted to look me over?"

"Precisely."

"Fine," I said, irritated. "And now that you're here, perhaps you'll tell *me* something. Why are you worried about Reva?"

"Eh? Oh, it's her finances, mostly. She's pretty reckless."

"You mean she's hard up?"

"She's not as well off as people think," Dunlop said sadly. "You see, her only actual property is the controlling block of shares in a night club—a wretched business, young man."

"What night club?"

"The Zebra. Her father established it years ago. He was a fine man, in spite of the business he was in. Well, he died a couple of years ago, leaving the Zebra to his widow, Reva's mother. She was a most charming woman, in spite of—"

"It was a bad business," I conceded. "But what happened?"

"Mrs. Savoy was a poor business woman. The night club appears to have been losing much money. Then Mrs. Savoy died, leaving it, in bad shape, to Reva."

"She doesn't manage it herself?"

"Oh, no. There's a manager. Rex Sturgis. A charming fellow. Mrs. Savoy liked him. But Sturgis is no good as a manager. It's a pity."

This fellow Dunlop puzzled me. It didn't seem likely that he would go to this trouble just to look me over because of his fatherly interest in Reva, yet it could be. And his frank and open discussion of Reva's affairs could be a smart way of getting my confidence, or it could be genuine.

"What's your business, Dunlop?" I said.

He seemed startled. "My business? Why, I'm a sort of a capitalist, in a small way. I'm president of the Dunlop Chemical Company. I also hold directorships in a few other companies."

"What other companies?"

"Oh, financial concerns, mostly." Amos Dunlop was looking at me sharply, as if he had just conceived a degree of respect for me. Then his look became bland and he said: "I must leave now. I only hope, for Reva's sake, that you're trustworthy."

He wiggled out of his chair. I took him to the landing and watched him waddle down the stairs. The street door banged after him.

"Now what the devil was the old coot *really* after?" I muttered.

I didn't leave the apartment until nearly four o'clock. I had an old Buick sedan in a shabby garage in a courtyard at the back of the building. The shaky sliding door was open about a foot. I stopped a moment, reflecting that I had left it open, all right, but not quite that much. I had had some trouble closing it, on account of a rusty hinge, and I remembered just about how I had left it.

I shoved the door all the way open. The car was parked back end inside, since it was easier to back into the garage than to drive in nose first.

I saw nothing out of the way in the garage, but I had an uneasy feeling that I should give things a more thorough scrutiny. However, I was anxious now to get out to the track.

The drive took me about thirty-five minutes.

CHAPTER III

Adams' Atom

THE huge parking grounds at the track were almost full, but not quite. I parked on the outer fringe of the great mass of cars. I trudged the long walk to the admittance gates, bought a ticket and a program, and pushed through the turnstiles.

The sixth race was run. The luckier ticket-holders were still jostling their way back toward the cashier's windows, and I came out of a tunnel to a spot between the main grandstand and the clubhouse section.

I stopped there, and looked over the heads of the mass of humanity in front of me. The big totalizator board was stretched along on the inner side of the track.

I watched that tote board.

Already, the figures being wagered on the seventh race were being reflected on the board. Reva Savoy's choice, Number three, was a long shot, all right. At the start of the wagering it was sixty to one.

My fingertips tingling, I fingered the

eleven hundred-dollar bills in my pocket. One of them was mine. I wondered if I should keep it, or plunk it on Number Three to win, along with Reva's thousand dollars.

When you're short of cash, as I was, a hundred bucks is nice to have. And sixty to one odds at least indicates that there are fifty-nine out of sixty chances to lose.

The minutes slipped by. The figures on the board were constantly changing. At seven minutes to five the odds on Number Three were down a little—fifty-six to one. Someone, apparently, was laying a little cush on Adams' Atom, but not enough to beat down the odds much.

I turned then and strode down the ramp. I had noticed a hundred-dollar selling window just under the grandstand. There was only one customer at the window. He moved away as I followed in line.

I shoved my money under the barrier.

"Eleven tickets on Number Three," I said.

The machine clicked out eleven tickets and the teller pushed them at me. I picked them up in fingers fumbling with excitement, and inserted them in an inner coat pocket.

I stepped away from the window.

A man stepped up, sidled against me. I looked at him sharply. He was short, stockily, yet neatly built. His face was heavily lined. The eyes were gray, steadfast. The mouth, in spite of its fullness, was firm.

"You're Walt Bonner," he said.

"You seem to know."

"Sure. I'm Jack Adams. You've just bet on my nag. Reva phoned me to watch out for you."

I felt annoyed again. "I guess I can't blame her for making sure about things. How did you know what window to watch?"

"I didn't know, but there ain't many hundred-dollar windows. I just took a chance."

"So did I," I said wryly. "On your horse. I put a hundred on him to win—my own money. Do I lose it?"

Adams shrugged. "Anything can happen. You know that. If the Atom doesn't get a last-minute stomachache, I think he'll make it. That's all."

"Sure. Well, I want to see this one."

Adams smiled wanly. "It means plenty to me," he said. "This is the minute I've been shooting at for years." There was strain in the gray eyes. "Well, see you in town tonight, maybe."

He turned and walked abruptly away. I walked up the ramp again just as the bugle blew for the seventh race.

I stood there motionless, numbed with excitement, and watched the horses emerge from the path; watched them skitter around until they were all set; watched them shoot out as the starter gave the sign; watched them scamper around the first turn.

A little horse named Adams' Atom was in that field. Number three. I couldn't see him, although my vision was perfect, but I knew he was there. Three people had bet money on him to win, and probably nobody else except, perhaps, for a few idle betters who might play a long-shot just for the heck of it.

With the horses already pounding along the back stretch, I felt vaguely amazed that it took so short a time for a horse race. Now they were around the far turn, most of them bunched, fighting for position. I closed my eyes, and would have closed my ears if I could.

THE roar of the crowd billowed up thunderously. Then, suddenly, the tumult softened into a mere babble.

I knew then that the race was over. I grinned as I opened my eyes, jeering at myself for my lack of nerve.

Feverishly, my gaze strayed to the tote board.

There it was! I yelped in spite of myself. Number Three had won!

The odds? The board said a two-dollar ticket was worth a hundred and eight dollars and forty cents.

I ignored the fractions and figured fast. Somewhat I forgot about my own winnings. I was thinking of Reva. Her thousand dollars was now worth about fifty-four thousand!

I rubbed my hand carelessly against the pocket that contained the tickets. They were there, all right.

Part of the crowd, I noticed, was already leaving, not caring for the eighth race. That suited me, too. I had no more interest in horse racing. I walked swiftly down the ramp, hurried past the paddock and out through the gate by which I had entered. My long-legged pace took me well ahead of all others. I made time down the long walk between thousands of parked cars.

I swerved then across to the corner where my car was parked. Still a bit feverish, I yanked open the door next to the wheel. I had one foot on the running board, and my head was in the car, when I froze.

Slumped in the back seat, blood streaking his face and neck, his eyes fishlike in chill death, was a little man dressed in a sporty green outfit.

I stared pensively at the ex-stable man, Chet Martin. Thoughts raced wildly through my mind. I could think of only one thing—that I certainly didn't want to get tangled up with the police right now, not when I knew so little about Reva Savoy's connections.

And obviously there was no time to try to figure out who had killed Martin, or why.

In a row of parked cars just ahead an old Ford and a sumptuous Packard stood side by side. I picked the Packard. It was nasty work. I had to carry the dead man cradled in my arms. I dumped the body on the floor of the Packard, slammed the door shut, and hurried back to my own car.

As I rounded my car, I caught sight of something on the back of it that puzzled me. But I couldn't stop then because a big man in tweeds appeared suddenly from the walk beyond and almost ran me down.

The big man, puzzled and slightly angry, stopped to watch me as I slipped in behind the wheel and backed the car out. He turned to stroll toward the Packard as I roared away.

A few miles along the highway, I turned off into a side road and stopped.

There were liberal blood-stains, I had noticed, on the back seat. And on the upper left of my gabardine coat, just under the lapel, was a splotch of blood that stood out like a big round button at a Rotarian's convention.

I took off my coat, in spite of the cold air, folded it neatly, and laid it on the back seat, over the blood stains.

Then I drove on.

The evening was chill as I drove into the blinking lights of the city. I stopped just off Main Street, got out, and walked into the nearest second-hand store.

When I came out again, I was wearing a tight-fitting brown coat, and there was a .32 automatic in my hip pocket.

I returned to my car, slipped in the back seat, took a quick look at the pedestrians on the sidewalk, then fished eleven tickets out of the gabardine coat pocket and transferred them to the one I was wearing.

The mere possession of those tickets made me nervous. They were so anonymous. They just belonged to anyone who was able to get his hands on them. There was absolutely nothing to show that they belonged to Reva, or to anyone else.

I got out of the car again, locked it, and walked across the street and into a cheap café.

At a back table, I ate a tough steak and thought about Reva Savoy. I wished I knew her better. About all I knew was that she was a knock-out and had a queer effect on me, and that she was now worth fifty-four thousand dollars in tote tickets—if I could get the tickets to her.

I GOT up presently and went to a wall phone in an alcove near the kitchen door. I had to do a lot of thumbing through the directory. And it took three calls to get the number of the man I wanted.

The voice was raspy, but with oil around the edges:

"Tom Tilson speaking."

"Hi, Tom," I said. "This is Walt Bonner."

"Walt!" The voice became cordial. "Didn't know you were back in town. What's on your mind?"

I sneered, but not out loud. Tom Tilson, night club columnist, evidently didn't know that I was no longer the reckless son of a lush father, as in prewar days. Tilson never had any use for either has-beens or want-to-be's. He was, in short, a snob.

"Oh, I'm just looking around," I said. "Thinking of going to work."

Tilson laughed. "You work?"

"Well, I've got to do something. Thought I'd make an investment."

"What kind of an investment?"

"A good night club might suit me."

"Ah. Got any in mind?"

"You know the Zebra, don't you?"

"The Zebra, eh?" Tilson said cautiously. "Well, there's something queer about that."

"What's queer about it?"

"The darned joint should clean up a hundred thousand a year. Gets a big play. Yet it consistently shows a loss, or so I've been told."

"How about the manager, Rex Sturgis?"

"Sturgis is a dope," snapped Tilson.

Anyhow, I thought, Tilson agreed with a respectable Amos Dunlop in his estimate of Sturgis.

"I'll look into it," I said.

"Okay, Walt. If you do anything about it, let me know."

"Sure."

I hung up, paid my check, and went out to the car. I started to get in, thought of something, then walked around to the rear of the car.

A cross had been marked, in chalk, on the back of the car, just above the bumper. This was what had caught my eye just before I left the race track. The lines of the cross were about six inches long.

I looked up to see a man standing on the curb, staring at me.

Casually—I hoped—I got in the car. I sat at the wheel and squinted at the card Reva had given me with her address on it. It was out toward the Rossland district, about twenty minutes' drive. Plenty of time. I drove slowly.

Reva's house was on a wide residential street where there was little traffic. The building was white stucco, pleasant but unpretentious, of two stories. I drove past it, made a U-turn, came back and parked across the street.

I had about five minutes. I sat in the car, waited and watched. Nothing happened. It was quiet. Apparently there were four apartments in the building, two downstairs and two up.

At one minute to eight, I crossed the street. I stood outside the four doors that were grouped in a semicircle. Reva's apartment was 1-A. I could see light beyond the frosted glass. I pressed the door button.

Almost instantly, the door lock clicked. I grasped the knob, pushed in. Four steps up led to a narrow carpeted corridor. I stood at the foot of the steps and peered along the corridor. Off the corridor were two doors, both closed. At the end of it, about ten paces, was a set of drapes which apparently hung over another doorway.

There was no sign of anyone.

"Reva?" I called.

There was no answer.

It wasn't right, and I hesitated. Then, deliberately, I walked up the steps and started along the corridor.

Five paces, and I halted. My hand went to my hip pocket. It came out just as the glint I had noticed at the side of the drapes blazed at me. The bullet sang past my head as I ducked. I fired, dropping to one knee. One more shot came at me, tore through my hat. I fired again.

Then there was silence.

LIKE a sprinter, I shot forward at the drapes, low. The hanging velvet yielded, and just beyond I crashed into a wall.

Stunned, I shook myself and stood erect. I was in partial darkness. I yanked at the drapes to let in the light.

I was standing at an open window. I looked out. Here was an indentation in the building's side wall. Someone was just vanishing around the back of the building.

I heard a car start. Then it was quiet again. There was an oppressive emptiness about the place. I moved back into the corridor, stood there, frowning. It was pure luck that I was alive. Someone had stood there, outside the window, and fired at me. The fellow outside had been in a fairly safe spot. His only disadvantage was that the drapes had hindered his vision.

The button that controlled the door lock was in the wall within inches of the drapes. The would-be killer had easily reached in through the window and pushed it.

But where was Reva?

I opened both doors, one after the other. The rooms beyond were unlighted. The whole apartment, obviously, was in darkness, except for the corridor.

Rapidly, I walked through rooms, switching on lights. Living room, dining room, bedroom, kitchen, bathroom. No sign of Reva, of anyone.

I sank into a chair in the living room. I got up again, quickly. Someone was insistently pushing the front door bell.

CHAPTER IV

Missing Lady

NOW I didn't bother with the button in the corridor, but just strode along to the front door. I stared at the door for a moment, uncertain. Then I pulled it open.

Just outside was the horseman, Jack Adams.

Adams' eyes narrowed. "I told Reva I'd be here," he said.

"Come in," I said.

We walked back to the living room. I could somehow feel the hard skepticism of the man beside me as he looked about.

"Where is she?" he asked.

"I don't know," I said.

His eyes glinted brightly. "What do you mean?"

"Reva told me to be here at eight o'clock," I said. "I was. And someone tried to kill me." I told Adams exactly what had happened, and added, "You can probably check the bullet-holes in the corridor. Two of 'em."

"And how do I know you didn't fire those shots yourself?" said Adams.

I shrugged. "You don't. But you'd better take my word for it." I took a good look at him. "You know Reva much better than I. Where do you think she could be?"

"She should be here. I don't know where else."

"Any idea who might know?"

"No."

"How about Amos Dunlop?" I said.

"Dunlop? I don't know. He's not a pal of mine." Adams' tone was still cold, suspicious. "He might know something. The old money-bags has always kept tab on Reva. Not that I blame him much for that. She needs a financial manager."

I walked over to the telephone, resting on a stand in the corner. I located a number in the directory, dialed it.

Dunlop's voice came soon. I told him who was calling.

"Have you seen Reva today?" I asked.

"I talked with her on the phone this morning, as I told you. I've had no further contact. Why?"

"I had a date to meet her at her apartment at eight o'clock. I'm here, but she isn't."

"Tut," said Dunlop fussily. "That's not like Reva."

"Probably nothing serious," I said, but not believing it.

"I hope not. Indeed, so. Sorry I can't help."

"Thanks."

I dropped the receiver, turned to Adams. "How about Sid Towne?"

"Towne might know something. He's been sticking pretty close to Reva lately. Curse him."

"So you don't like him?"

"I wouldn't trust him," said Adams, "within seven furlongs of a manure pile."

I dialed another number. With luck, I thought, I might reach Towne at the hotel. The luck was with me. Towne was in his room.

"I'm Walt Bonner. Remember?"

"Of course." There was no friendly note in Towne's voice.

"I'm looking for Reva," I said. "Know where she is?"

"No."

"When did you see her last?"

"Just before she tricked me, late this afternoon," Towne snapped.

"What do you mean, tricked you?"

"We went to a picture show—the Summers Theatre. It was Reva's idea. The second feature was nearly over when she got up and went back up the aisle. She told me she'd be back in ten or fifteen minutes. I thought she'd just gone to the rest room." Sid Towne took time to swear lustily, and finished, "She never came back. I haven't seen her since."

Queer, I thought. If true, of course. Then something popped in the idea section of my skull.

"What time did all this happen?" I said.

"About a quarter to five," grumbled Towne.

"Well, thanks," I said. "I just thought—"

"Now, look," cut in Towne. "Let *me* ask *you* something."

"Okay."

"Why," Towne said ominously, "did you break into my hotel room this morning?"

I took a moment to handle that. "You mean someone broke into your room, and you think it was me?"

"Yes. When I went back up to my room, just before taking Reva to the show, I found that the contents of my desk had been disturbed."

"Was something missing?"

"You should know," Towne said cagily.

"I could make a rough guess," I said, and hung up.

JACK Adams had been watching me stonily. I told him Towne's story.

"Towne is a liar," said Adams.

"You mean you don't believe it happened like that?"

"I just mean I don't believe anything Towne says."

Well, I myself didn't know who to believe. Nor how much. I seemed to be getting the pattern of things in a hazy sort of way, but so far nothing fitted together any too snugly. There was Chet Martin getting killed in my car. And someone trying to kill me out there in the corridor. It was pretty hard to figure the connection. And what had happened to Reva Savoy?

I ignored Adams' hard, unbelieving eyes and started walking round the room, poking into things. Presently I sat down at an old-fashioned secretary and rummaged through the drawers. Adams sat immovable in his chair.

"You have no right to do that," he said.

I was now busy reading a document. "When people shoot at me," I said, without turning, "I've got a right to do practically anything."

I went on reading. It was a legal document. I gathered from the involved terminology that Reva Savoy had put her block of stock in the Zebra Corporation in hock, that the mortgage was held by the Central Finance Co., and that the mortgage, already extended, had to be met by July 17, which was just two days hence.

The amount was thirty-five thousand dollars, plus interest.

I put the document back and looked through more.

There seemed to be nothing else that mattered.

I swung around and said: "How about you and me going out to that night club, the Zebra?"

"I'm staying right here," he said firmly.

"You know where it is?"

"A few blocks beyond Vermont and a couple of blocks north of Beverly."

"So I'll go myself."

"Why?"

"Just fishing for a lead," I said. "Reva has an interest in the place. No doubt she goes there sometimes."

Adams shifted in his seat. "How

[*Turn page*]

about giving me Reva's tote tickets. I'll give them to her when I see her."

"No."

"I was afraid you wouldn't." The horseman's low voice was brittle, hostile. "By the way, there was a murder out at the track this afternoon, at the edge of the parking grounds. A fellow who used to work for me was killed. It happened about the time you left the track. You don't happen to know about that?"

Well, I wasn't going to get tangled up in that now.

"No," I said, and walked out. . . .

The Zebra was a place of semiconcealed magnificence with an ornate atmosphere of subdued luxury. However, I didn't care about how the dump looked. I just strolled past a suspicious doorman and approached a liveried flunky in the main foyer.

I said I wanted to see the manager, Rex Sturgis. The flunky looked me up and down and said he thought Mr. Sturgis was busy, and what did the man want?

I didn't tell him. I turned and walked up thickly carpeted stairs to my left, and came onto a hallway. There were two doors up here. I opened one of them and the room beyond was dark. I opened the next one, and there were two men in a pleasantly furnished office.

I walked in.

The man who was standing stared at me, curiously. The man who was sitting at a desk arose abruptly and said nervously:

"Who are you? What do you want?"

A handsome fellow, this Rex Sturgis. Almost offensively handsome. His features were delicately pointed, and flawlessly regular. There was a semi-circular streak of gray in the wide wave of his dark hair. His voice was a high tenor, but soft.

ENTIRELY different was the man with Sturgis. He was of medium height, and knobby-shouldered. He had flaring nostrils and shifty firefly eyes.

"I'm looking for Reva Savoy," I said.

"Reva?" Sturgis was uncomfortable. "I haven't seen her for a couple of days. She doesn't come here much."

"She seems to be missing," I said.

"Missing?" Sturgis blinked helplessly, and turned to the other fellow. "Have you seen Reva today, Archie?"

"No," said the man, as if he were in a great hurry to deny something.

I looked at him and said: "Who the devil are you?"

He scowled. "What's it to you?"

"Don't be juvenile, Archie," put in Sturgis. He told me, "This is Archie Ford. He's employed here in a confidential capacity."

"Meaning he's a house cop?"

"Call it that, if you like."

"So I'll call it that." I was watching this Archie Ford. "Haven't I seen you somewhere?"

Ford's eyes moved away. "I don't think so."

I studied him, hard. "Maybe I haven't seen you," I said. "Let's put it this way: haven't *you* seen *me* somewhere?"

"No."

I didn't believe that. Archie Ford was much too anxious. And the way his eyelids kept shielding his eyes indicated he was lying.

I noticed that he was constantly consulting his wrist watch. An engagement to keep, perhaps?

"I'd better get on the job," he said abruptly to Sturgis.

"All right, Archie."

He hurried out. If it was an engagement, I thought, it would be for ten o'clock, since the small clock on the desk said one minute to ten.

Sturgis was turned away as if he didn't want to look at me.

"I'm Walt Bonner," I said. "Reva Savoy employed me—also in a confidential capacity."

"You—you have credentials?"

"I could have," I said. "I understand she is the largest stockholder in this joint. Who are the other stockholders?"

Sturgis was silent a minute, as if debating a problem with himself. Finally he said: "There are only three—Fred Crowther, Jake Wetzel and Sid Towne."

"How about yourself?"

"I have one share of stock. Just a matter of form."

Well, of the three others, I knew only one—Sid Towne.

"Is Towne a heavy stockholder?" I said.

"Oh, no. Sid has only a small interest."

"Have you seen him this evening?"

"No." Sturgis frowned. "Sid phoned an hour or so ago. He asked about Reva. Said he'd be out here later."

"He did, eh? And what—"

"I'm very busy, Mr. Bonner," cut in Sturgis. "Furthermore, I have no evidence that you are a bona fide representative of Miss Savoy. Get out!"

I went close to him, stared down into his face.

"Look, Sturgis," I said. "They say you're a fool. I think you're also a crook! You've been running this business into the red, and somebody must pay you to do that."

Sturgis flinched. "Get out!" his voice squeaked.

"And I can name your secret employer!" I said.

Sturgis tried to say something, but his vocal chords got all tangled up and he almost strangled. I thought it was time to be going. I grinned at the fellow and walked out. I closed the door, but not quite.

I hoped Sturgis, in his agitation, wouldn't notice that the door was open about half an inch.

He didn't notice it. He was frantically calling a telephone number, and I thought I recognized the number. I waited, quietly. Sturgis seemed to be in trouble, and presently, unable to get his number, he crashed the receiver back into the cradle.

CHAPTER V

Assorted Corpses

CREEPING away from the door, I strolled along the corridor and went down to the foyer. I walked out of the main exit, and stood out front for a little while, watching.

I had started away, headed for the parking lot, when I heard the shot.

The sound seemed muffled; not by distance, but by the building itself.

I ran around the south side of the building in a great hurry and stopped outside a small rear door. A small faint light glimmered over the door. The light failed to reach the small private parking lot nearby, but it did fall dimly into the alcove near the door.

The man who was lying there was dead. He seemed to have been shot in the temple. Blood pulsed out messily. I recognized him easily, having seen him just a few minutes before—Archie Ford, the night club's private cop.

No one else had reached there yet. I got down beside the body. There had been a suspicion in my mind. I found Ford's gun in his holster, so he certainly hadn't fired it. I broke it open. There were six chambers, four of them loaded.

My suspicion became a certainty—at least in my own mind.

Then came a rush of others. I got up and found Sturgis right behind me.

"It's your man Ford," I said. "I had an idea he came out here to meet someone."

Sturgis, his face as pallid as skimmed milk, only shuddered. He seemed to be shrinking back, as much from me as from the dead man.

That forced a laugh out of me.

"I didn't do it," I said. I slipped my own gun out and prodded the air with it under Sturgis' nose. "My gun hasn't been fired. Take a sniff of it."

Instead of sniffing, Sturgis yelped and backed away.

It was, I thought, high time to be moving away from there. I walked quickly away into the darkness and located my car. . . .

Back at Reva Savoy's apartment, I rang the door bell, and waited a moment. There was no response. I tried the door. It was unlocked and I walked in. The corridor was lighted. So was the living room.

But Jack Adams was not there.

I sat down and wondered about Adams. Then I wondered about Reva Savoy, much more intently. It was clear that Reva had either played a weird trick on several people—especially on me—or she was in a tough spot. She might even be dead.

The crucial time, it seemed to me, was when—if Sid Towne had been telling the truth—she had deserted Towne in the theatre. Why had she left the theatre? I thought I could answer.

But what had happened to her? I could only guess at that.

And where was she now? I hadn't the slightest idea.

I was sitting like a crude reproduction of The Thinker when I heard the front door lock click. Someone was walking quietly along the corridor, had appeared at the living room door.

Then I was looking at the gray, grim face of Jack Adams. Motionless, he stared at me out of bloodshot eyes.

"Been somewhere?" I said.

Adams blew something like a sigh through rigid lips and moved into the room. He stood against the wall.

"Yes," he said. "I drove down town. I went to take a look at the Summers Theatre."

"Ah," I said. Adams could, I thought, be lying, but I had no good reason to think so. "That was a good idea. What did you find out?"

"Nothing. The theatre is practically in the business district, surrounded by office buildings and stores."

"No cocktail lounges?"

"Not within a couple of blocks." Adams' eyes were puzzled. "Why should Reva sneak out for a cocktail?"

"I don't think she would, either." I took one of Reva's cigarettes from a container on the table beside me. "You seem to be taking this very seriously, Adams."

"Maybe so," Adams said huskily. "I'm fond of that girl. And her father—well, he practically saved my neck, financially. He was one of the best. That's why I let her in on that race this afternoon."

"Sure." I lit the cigarette. "How about Sid Towne?"

"What about him?"

"Is he a horse bettor?"

"Yeah," said Adams. "A heavy plunger, when he thinks he's got a good thing."

"Reva didn't tell you why she didn't go out to the track this afternoon?"

"No."

ABRUPTLY, I shifted the line of inquiry.

"It's queer about those two guys getting shot."

Adams stiffened. "Two?"

"Oh, didn't you know? Yes. You knew about Chet Martin, this afternoon. Then there was Archie Ford, not long ago." I peered at Adams through the smoke. "There seems to be no connection, but there certainly must be. Both of them shot in the head, too. The killer must be a one-method operator."

"If the same guy killed 'em both," said Adams.

I nodded agreement. "The point is, why should anyone kill either of them?"

Adams eyed me queerly. "You don't know, huh?"

"I don't know. But I've been making guesses. Did you know Archie Ford?"

"Not good."

"But you knew Chet Martin well."

"Sure. Crooked as a dog's hind leg, Chet was. I wouldn't trust him from here out, in any direction." Adams frowned. "Funny thing about Chet Martin, though."

"What was funny about him?"

"Well, crooked as he was, he was crazy about Reva."

"H'm. You mean, in a romantic way?"

"Maybe. Anyway, Reva was tops with him. Not that he expected anything. She was way out of his class."

"That may be important," I said thoughtfully. "And that other guy, Archie Ford—what were his relations with Reva?"

Adams squinted. "Ford? I don't think Reva had much to do with him. I've heard her mention him. I think he drove her around sometimes, acted as chauffeur for her."

I sat up straight. "Well, well," I said. "As a private detective I guess I need a few more lessons. I should have asked you these things before, Adams. So Archie Ford drove Reva around, eh?"

"Yes," Adams said. "In a car belonging to the night club. A big limousine."

"In what?"

"In a big car belonging to the Zebra. I heard it was Rex Sturgis' idea, buying the limousine."

"So Ford drove—"

The telephone bell tinkled pleasantly. I looked across at the telephone. It tinkled again. I saw Adams start that way, so I got up and hurried and beat him to it. I lifted the receiver.

"Hello," I said.

"Is this Mr. Bonner?" said a quiet, soft voice.

"Yes."

"This is Arthur Detman. You remember me? I met you at the McBains' party."

Detman . . . Arthur Detman . . . Gradually the name and the voice brought into focus the clear picture of a little man in a blue-black suit; a very neat, precise, courteous little man with a little pot belly; the man I had seen coming out of the hotel in the morning when I had been going in.

"Oh, yes," I said.

"That's good of you," said Mr. Detman, gratefully. "Is Mr. Adams with you?"

"Yes."

"Good. Please give him a message. You don't need to call him to the phone."

"But he's right here."

"Don't bother to call him. This is the message. Tell him that I just saw Miss Savoy, and she said—"

"You saw her! Where?"

"Near the Heathers Hotel," Detman said. "I just happened to meet her. She seemed agitated, but I don't know why. She wanted me to call her apartment, and if Mr. Adams was there he was to go at once to the hotel and meet her where she met you, over in the far corner of the lobby."

"Look, Detman," I said. "Why didn't Reva phone here herself?"

"I really don't know, except that she seemed to think she was being watched. She spoke to me furtively, in a low voice." I could distinctly hear the little man sigh. "It's all very puzzling."

"But," I said, "I'd rather you told Adams yourself. He's right here, I told you."

BUT Detman had hung up. I swung around. Adams was watching me dubiously.

I gave him the message. Adams seemed stunned.

"Is—is this on the level?"

"I'm only telling you what the man said," I said wearily. "Are you going down to the hotel?"

He shrugged helplessly. "What else can I do? If Detman is telling the truth, Reva wouldn't want me to phone and have her paged. And I don't dare take a chance on it being phony. It could be straight stuff."

"It could be, yes."

"You're staying here?"

I thought about it for a long moment. "Yes, I'll stay here. You can phone me from the hotel."

Adams stood rigid. I could see what he was up against. He had to go, yet he hated to leave me.

Then he swerved rapidly and was gone. I heard the sharp slam of the street door.

It was quiet in the flat; very quiet. I sat quite still and thought about the little man, Arthur Detman. I certainly didn't know much about him. He had some kind of an office of his own somewhere, Reva had said.

On the other hand, he could be a prize snooper for some weightier brain.

My hands, I noticed then, were moist, and the moisture was cold. My nerves were singing a weird tune that was hammering at my ears.

Well, I was pretty sure I knew now who had killed Martin and Ford, knew who was doing these things and why, and I knew what had happened to Reva at five o'clock in the afternoon.

But I didn't know where Reva was now. That was the weak spot. That was what tied me down. That was why all I could do was sit there and wait.

CHAPTER VI

SET FOR THE FINAL ACT

LOTS of things could happen in twenty minutes, I thought. And it would take Adams about twenty minutes to reach the hotel.

I moved only to light another cigarette. I was sitting facing the open living room door. The minutes sped on—five minutes, ten, fifteen.

I heard nothing. And in spite of myself, and of all I had been thinking, I felt surprised presently to find myself looking at the man who was standing in the doorway.

A neat little man in a blue-black suit. His pale eyes gleamed in a shriveled face. And even the gun in Arthur Detman's bony little hand seemed neat and trim, and steady.

I felt a sudden choking constriction in my chest. There was something fanatical, something deadly, about this little man with the little gun.

I cleared my throat loudly. "You surprise me, Detman. And yet I expected you."

"You knew I was coming?"

"I wasn't dead sure, but it seemed likely." I looked up at him. "You phoned here with a message for Adams, but you failed to explain how you knew I was here."

Detman's face was grave but unworried. "I had to take a chance you wouldn't think of that. And of course Jack Adams can't say for sure that I phoned here. I didn't talk to him."

"I can see that." The inference was that I wasn't going to be able to talk, anyway. "I wondered at first why you told me your name, why you didn't make the call anonymous, or fake a name. And then I realized you had to give your name, otherwise Adams and I would have known it was a trick." I laughed, but not heartily. "I was pretty sure it was a trick, anyway—a trick to get me alone."

"You knew, and yet you stayed?"

"Sure. Because I had to meet a killer. And I figured this for the final act. It is, isn't it?"

"Oh, yes."

"By the way, how did you get in here?"

"There's a back door to this apartment."

I nodded. "By the way, Detman, I got accused of something this morning that I think you did."

"What was that?"

"Breaking into Sid Towne's hotel room."

"Really?"

"Yes." I looked him over speculatively, but without hope. The fellow was immovable, and incredibly alert. "You seem to be waiting for something."

"Yes. For just a little while."

"I guess Reva's block of stock in that night club started the trouble," I said, to fill in the time.

"Indeed?" Detman was indifferent.

"I think so. The night club was losing money, yet the place is a potential money-maker. That was because Sturgis, the manager, under orders from somewhere else, deliberately upped the expense, probably by spending too much for high-class entertainment.

"So this someone planned to acquire Reva's stock. She had borrowed money on it, and if she failed to pay it off in the next day or two she would lose it to the finance company. And then this someone would be in a position to bid it in cheap from the finance company.

"But there was a hitch. Reva could make the money in two minutes on a horse race. Of course it was a long shot, but still possible. And that wouldn't do at all. In fact, it probably drove the scheming crook crazy, thinking that the whole deal might slip through his hands at the last minute because of a lucky bet. Well, he was having Reva watched closely. There was Chet Martin and Archie Ford and you—"

"I?"

"Certainly, you. You're just a spying tool, Detman."

"Perhaps." Detman was suddenly brisk. "It's time now. You will get up carefully, Bonner, keeping your hands stretched in front of you. You will walk out here to the corridor, turn right, and then through another door into the kitchen, and out of the back door."

WELL, I had a gun in my pocket. It would probably be suicide to reach for it. And anyhow I wanted to get past Detman to the man behind him. I wanted to go right along to the end of this trail of murder.

And I wanted, desperately, to see Reva Savoy.

So I got up and moved, precisely as I was told. Soon I was past Detman, and he was behind me. Along the corridor, through the kitchen, and out into the dark and night-chilled yard at the back of the building.

One door of the large black limousine

swung open.

"Get in," Detman said in a whisper.

I inclined my lengthy body and thrust my head into the car's rear section. I caught just a glimpse of Reva Savoy, huddled in a corner.

I saw no more. Something cracked hard against the back of my skull. . . .

There was no gun in my pocket when the torture in my head shoved me back into consciousness. I was lying on my side, and there was no hard bulge against my thigh.

And there were no tote tickets in my inner coat pocket. I felt for them right away.

Another thing I noticed, before I moved my head, was a thing about four feet long that looked like a section of pipe. It was fitted snugly between the car wall and the back of the front seat, as if someone were anxious to keep it from jolting.

I couldn't see it well, though; it was too dark, and anyway I wasn't seeing anything well at the moment.

My head was pillowed against something pleasantly soft. That was Reva, of course.

I forced my head up, like lifting an iron ball on a feather. And there was Arthur Detman.

The little man was kneeling on the front seat, facing me and Reva. His gun was still in his hand, as if it had always been there, as if it were a part of the hand. Detman's eyes were as immovable as the gun itself.

I turned my head. Yes, here was Reva. Her arms and legs were bound with rope, but she was not gagged. Come to find out, my arms and legs were bound the same way; around the wrists and ankles. There was a half-smile on Reva's face. She had nothing to smile about, though.

The car was moving, going up grade. To the left, I could see the side of a hill. To the right, far off, and below, was a vast pattern of city lights.

The silence impressed me. It was soundless in the car. The windows, of course; heavy closed windows that killed noise.

"Are you all right, Walt?" Reva said.

Her voice was low and steady. Yet I knew she was badly shaken, that fear had frozen that faintly bitter smile on her face.

"I'm okay," I said, and I tried to keep my voice down, yet it seemed to reverberate in the flat silence of the car.

"Still on business, of course," she said mockingly.

I didn't answer that. Detman, I noticed, seemed quite without interest in the conversation, intent only on seeing that we didn't move.

My eyes shifted then to the man behind the wheel. I could tell little about him. The brim of the man's felt hat was pulled low, secretively. The collar of his overcoat was turned up to his ears. His head was motionless, face steadfastly forward.

"You should have told me about Sid Towne," I said.

Reva sighed gently. "Perhaps I should have. But, you see, while I liked you on sight, I didn't know you well. I just thought it would be safer not to talk. Anyhow, I'd promised Jack Adams to be careful and not to let anyone else know."

"So I figured. You didn't want Towne to know about that long-shot. He knew something was coming up, but didn't know when. He wanted to be in on it. You didn't go out to the track yourself because you didn't want to tip him off. You not only stayed in town, but even kept him with you."

REVA sighed wearily.

"Yes," she said simply.

"You wanted to keep Sid Towne in the dark," I said, "for the good reason that if he had known he would have put heavy dough on Adam's Atom's nose, which would have made the odds sag and cost you plenty."

"Yes."

"So you went to the show with him. Just before five o'clock, you left the theatre. Why? Well, the seventh race was run at five. You'd be anxious to know how it finished. You merely went out to get the race returns on the radio."

"Of course."

"But where would you listen? There's no place handy to the theatre. So you had Archie Ford waiting for you in the car—this car—outside the theatre. You could listen to the car radio, riding around the block. Then you could go back in."

"So I thought." Reva shivered. "But it didn't work out that way. Ford and Detman were both in the car, and before I knew it they had kidnaped me."

My eyes were working better now. That thing that looked like a length of pipe, wedged in against the car wall, to my right—it wasn't a pipe at all. No, it was a walking cane.

I had never seen that cane before, though. It had a round knob on the top, and a faint indentation ran around the cane just below the knob.

I looked then at the back of the man who was driving.

"You were fooled by the one man you never suspected," I said to Reva.

"It just never occurred to me to suspect him."

"Yes. And he's in deep now. He probably never thought it would come to murder. But he had been so desperately intent on seizing your stock in the night club for so long that he just had to follow through, no matter what. He—"

The man behind the wheel had shifted a little. The car was slowing. There was no longer any sign of city lights. Bleak hillsides rose steeply on all sides. With great care, the man at the wheel brought the car to a stop.

The road here was much wider. And the car had been swung around so that it was nosed out toward the side of the road.

Its front wheels were within a few feet of a precipitous drop.

In my new profession, I reflected bitterly, I was pretty much of a failure. First, I had managed to figure out what had happened, except for what had happened to Reva.

Then I had found Reva. Here she was right beside me.

But what good did that do? Anyone with even half my brains could figure out what was about to come next—and soon.

The man at the wheel was turning around. His owlish eyes peered at me, and then they heard a low wheezing chuckle.

And Amos Dunlop said politely: "This is the end of the trail, my friends."

CHAPTER VII

Tickets to Perdition

DUNLOP'S hand appeared on the edge of the seat. He was holding a revolver. Without taking his eyes away from us, he said:

"I'll take care of 'em, Detman. You go get that other car."

I sat still. I had the uneasy feeling that if I so much as moved an inch, the jar would send the big car hurtling over the frail rim of that precipice.

Detman warily sidled out of the door nearest him, and vanished.

"Another car?" I said.

"Yes. Detman drove it up here several hours ago, as soon as I realized what had to be done. It is parked about a quarter of a mile away."

What had to be done! Well, that was no mystery.

Dunlop confirmed it by saying, regretfully: "Too bad to lose this beautiful car!"

"Does Detman know he's going to die, too?" I said sourly.

Dunlop seemed genuinely astonished. "Detman! Dear me, no! I have no fear of Detman. He's been my man for years, my discreet and reliable tool."

"That won't save him," I said, "when you begin to worry about him. Your one great fear is that someone doing your dirty work will, purposely or accidentally, betray you!"

Dunlop breathed a gusty sigh. "Yes. I confess that is always uppermost in my mind. I just can't permit that."

"Sure. Which is why you killed Martin and Ford."

"Ah. So you know that?"

"That's the only way this thing fits together. Chet Martin was up in my flat. I caught him there. I think he was just trying to get a line on me, for you, but he bungled the job. So you lost confidence in him. Also you were afraid he might weaken because of the way he felt about Reva.

"However, you came up to see me and kept me busy while Martin marked a cross on the back of my car. That was to make it easy to locate me out at the track. He was supposed to get those tote tickets from me, one way or another. But you didn't trust him any more. So you followed him out there and killed him, figuring you'd get the tote tickets later."

"You'd make a good detective, my friend—if you lived," Dunlop said admiringly.

"Nice of you," I said. "So then you had Archie Ford wait for me at Reva's flat. But he failed, too, and he had to go."

"How do you know it was Archie?"

"Well, I met him out at the Zebra. I knew I had never seen him before, yet I was sure from his reactions that *he* had seen *me*. A few minutes later, when I found him dead, I examined his gun and found two chambers empty, and the fellow at the apartment had fired at me twice. Just an indication, of course."

"But rather good," approved Dunlop.

"So Ford's failure wiped him up so far as you were concerned," I said. "Anyhow, he was a link connecting you with the whole set-up, and you were afraid to let him live. You met him by appointment back of the Zebra, and let him have it."

"You can prove this?"

I laughed, unhappily. "I could work evidence into proof. If you'd give me the time. Would you mind?"

Dunlop wagged his head. "I'm afraid I would." He cocked his head, listening. There was no sound of Detman in the other car; no sound from anywhere at all. "It is even disquieting," he went on, "that you suspected me at all."

"I hadn't much reason to suspect you," I said. "Except that you're crazy about money. But then I told Rex Sturgis I knew who was paying him to run the night club into the red, and he got the jitters and tried to get you on the phone. I was listening outside his door and recognized your number."

"That fellow Sturgis," muttered Dunlop, in pious disgust, "is a fool. I shall have to deal with him."

"Good night, Mr. Sturgis," I said.

The headlights of another car were now moving cautiously around the bend, coming toward us. The glare slashed through the windows and painted our faces a dull freakish yellow.

"This will be Detman," Dunlop said comfortably.

It was.

I GLANCED at Reva. A real thoroughbred, was Miss Savoy. I admired the cool lines of her face. Her eyes, though, seemed twice as large as normal.

"Sorry I got you into this, Walt," she said gently, aware of my scrutiny. "My fault entirely."

"Just business," I reminded her. "Think nothing of it."

Which was the sort of silly thing people say when they are trying to be nonchalant when the hand of death is touching them. She was thinking, plenty. So was I. Not that it did us any good at all. I hadn't the faintest idea what to do about it.

Then, strangely enough, I was looking at that walking cane, wondering about it. I managed to move my hands over, keeping them low, until my fingers touched it.

A light-weight thing, it seemed to me. Not heavy enough to stun a dog with, if you wanted to stun a dog, which I didn't.

A door latch clicked faintly. Arthur Detman stuck his head in. The placidity of his pale eyes in the shriveled face fascinated me.

"Everything is ready now, Mr. Dunlop," he said respectfully.

Amos Dunlop was motionless, just studying Reva and me as if making sure that everything was really ready.

"Yes," he said then. "Yes, I think so."

"Are you sure, Dunlop?" I said hurriedly. "Remember, if Reva and I are found in this thing with the doors locked, it won't be so good."

"Rest your mind on that," Dunlop said soothingly. "It's seven hundred feet to the rocks below." He chuckled. "No, we won't worry about locked doors."

There seemed to be an icicle resting along my brow. Nothing but a few beads of sweat, of course.

"But the ropes," I argued. "The ropes around our wrists and ankles. If we're found with the ropes still tied, it'll be a dead give-away!"

I held my breath. It seemed too much to expect that I could scare Dunlop into giving me a chance at him by cutting the ropes away.

I was right. It was too much to expect.

Dunlop only laughed. "I have already thought of that," he said.

"But what can you do?" I cried.

"Fire!" Dunlop said simply.

"Fire?"

"Yes. Fire inside the car. Fire, my friend, which will completely destroy the ropes and everything else in the car, and leave no trace!"

Hah! That kind of a fire! To a guy who had dropped incendiaries over Tokyo, that should mean something.

Reva was silent, intense. I could see tiny drops of moisture along her taut-drawn upper lip.

Then, again, I was looking at Dunlop's walking cane. It wasn't the same cane, I remembered, that I had seen him with when he first called at my flat. It was a different cane.

Now Dunlop was talking to Detman again.

"Just one thing more. That little pile of brush and driftwood under the front wheels. Pull the stuff out of the way so the car will move freely."

"Yes, sir."

Dunlop was still watching us. But I had a sudden fit of coughing that brought my head low. And my hands moved sideward. My wrists were bound tight, but my fingers were free.

When I straightened, the cane was between my knees. Grateful for the darkness, I nudged Reva with my knee.

"Tell this madman what you think of him—while you can," I said.

Reva caught her breath, as if pushing a sob back down her throat. But she spoke steadily, with calm fury. She poured out words at Amos Dunlop, without stopping for breath. And she kept on, even when I had another coughing spell.

My tingling fingertips had found a ridge around the cane, just below the knob. I tightened my fingers and twisted.

The knob unscrewed.

Then Detman's voice floated in through the car door:

"It's all right now, sir. A gentle push will send her over."

"Ah, good!"

AMOS Dunlop moved deliberately. He kept his gun in his right hand, and bent forward. His left hand dropped over the seat and fumbled toward the side.

"He wants his cane," I thought.

I had unscrewed the top and dropped it with a faint thud on the floor. I noticed that Dunlop was suddenly rigid with suspicion—no cane! I lifted the cane in my two hands and hurled it forward and out through the car door, as if I were throwing a dart, with the top end forward.

A few drops of water flicked against the car window.

The cane dropped outside, just beyond Detman.

Amos Dunlop seemed frozen stiff. Fear and rage blazed from his eyes. He was like an animal, cheated of its victim.

For a few moments there was utter silence.

I stared at the gun in Dunlop's hand. He would certainly use that gun now.

Then, with the explosive suddenness of a flash of lightning, a fierce fire seemed to spring from nowhere. And the sound of Detman's piercing scream raised the hair on my neck.

My two hands clenched in front of me, I lunged forward just as Dunlop fired. My doubled fist crashed into the face and sent him back against the dashboard.

The fire outside was burning with furious brilliance. Arthur Detman wasn't shrieking any more.

Awkwardly, I lifted myself up, flopped over into the front seat. Dunlop, squirmed around, was trying to use his gun. I smashed my knuckles into his face again. He slumped.

"Hurry!" I urged.

That fire was getting hotter, close to the car.

I helped Reva over into the front seat, shoved open the door on the wheel side. We both tumbled out. Sparks were shooting at the car from the other side.

I yanked hard at Dunlop's limp form,

until it was free of the wheel, tugged it out and across the road.

Well, first things come first. I hadn't forgotten what it was all about. I got down on my knees and searched Dunlop's pockets. I found a pocket knife and eleven pieces of pasteboard.

I used the knife to cut away our ropes. Then, without a word, I handed Reva ten of the tote tickets.

I put the eleventh one in my own pocket. . . .

We were pretty well played out, so we sat quietly against a big boulder, side by side, and said nothing, just watched the big car burn.

"It's okay by me, if it wants to burn," Reva said.

"You talk like you're going out of the night club business."

"I am, indeed. All I wanted was to get my stock out of hock so I could get a fair price for it."

That was none of my business. I kept my mouth shut.

And then Reva said: "That fire—what caused it?"

"A stick of phosphorus. Easy for Dunlop to get, being a chemist. Has to be kept under water, you know. Expose it to the air and it flares up in no time. He had a glass tube in that walking cane. The tube was filled with water, and the phosphorus was in that."

Reva shuddered. "If we'd gone over the cliff with that in the car—"

"We'd have been cinders," I said. "Just clinkers."

We were silent again. The fire started by the phosphorus was about gone. The burning car was smoldering.

"I think Detman went over," I said moodily.

"I didn't see him."

"He caught fire, lost his bearings and went over. He's down below."

"Poor fellow."

"My heart does not bleed," I said coldly. I pointed at Dunlop, still stretched out, still moaning. "I think that guy's busted something inside. I wouldn't say what in the presence of a lady."

"Sorry I got you into this, as I said before."

"Just business," I said.

"Only business, huh?"

"Certainly."

She shuddered again, more violently. "I'm a female in distress, and I'm not kidding."

"What am I supposed to do about it?"

"You might put your arm around me and kiss me, darn it."

"Okay, if you don't tell anyone."

I put an arm about her. I kissed her. I knew then that it wouldn't be the last time.

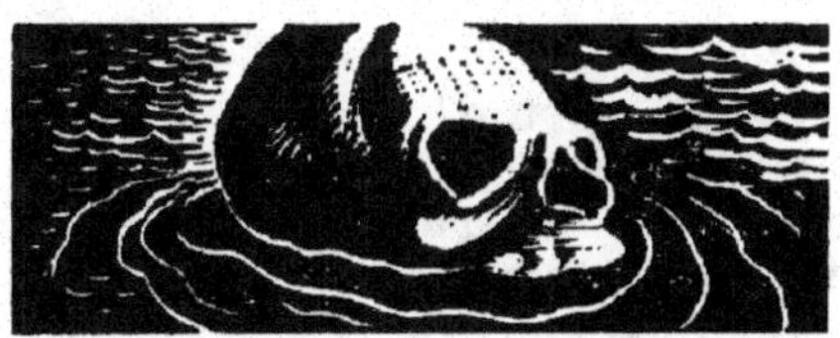

Washed ashore by the sea, the corpse of one of the Porter Twins becomes the focal point of a mystery packed with suspense—

HAUNT ME NO MORE

by

EDWARD RONNS

Next Issue's Featured Complete Novel

CREPE

a JOHNNY CASTLE novelet

CHAPTER I
Two Down

IT WAS one of those warm spring nights when everyone was going somewhere. I sat in a taxi with Libby Hart, bound for the Paladium. That was the block long amusement center, a stone's throw from Columbus Circle.

It was opening night at the Paladium.

A big ice pageant, called "The Frozen Follies of 1948," was due to unveil at eight-forty-five on the tick.

The star of the hard water carnival was Suzette Darcy. And Libby's interest in the skate *opus,* I happened to know, had to do with this same Miss Darcy.

Lib's sweatshop, which kept her in alligator shoes and free cosmetics, was known to the trade as Arcady House. The outfit manufactured first aids to fading faces. The girl friend did publicity and that's where Suzette Darcy floated in.

Arcady House, laying it on the line for an endorsement testimonial, was about to present Miss Darcy with a cash donation for her signed approval of Perfect Petal Cream, the emollient that made tired eyes pack their bags and leave.

Libby, handling the transaction, had a pair of Annie Oakleys in her purse. They were the reason for the taxi and the ice show.

As a sports writer for the *Orbit,* I should have been at the Garden watch-

FOR SUZETTE

When the gorgeous water carnival star is slain, racketeers warn Johnny to lay off the case—but there's a mystery to be solved!

Nick Caduro was holding a Colt automatic and it was leveled at my heart

by

C. S. MONTANYE

ing them toss a basketball around. But Lib had been insistent and so, fifteen minutes later, I sat down beside her in one of the choice boxes at the Paladium.

The place was filled to capacity. Park Avenue blended with the Bronx. Brooklyn rubbed elbows with Times Square. Three rows of standees were in the distant rear of the place.

It was just before curtain time. The lights were still up and I had a chance to a gander at the celebrities. They were as thick as Tuxedos at a waiters' convention.

In the next box I caught a glimpse of old Amos Tinsley. He was the millionaire, so-called "Flour King," formerly of St. Paul and points west. Tinsley had a droopy mustache, eyes to match and a fluff of snowy hair. He sat all alone, looking bored.

My gaze wandered. On the other side of our box I suddenly caught sight of two characters who made my brows lift. One was a shiny-haired, dark-faced man who wore his evening clothes with the air of an ambassador. He had very white, square teeth. He used them in a smile he turned on and off like a faucet.

BUT it wasn't hard to peg the polished gent. The label read, Nicholas Caduro.

I happened to know quite a lot about him. A big-time hot shot, gambler, strongarm and felony expert, Caduro didn't have one racket. He had them all. Wherever there was a loose dollar, Nick Caduro was present, reaching for it. A bad guy to meet up with under any conditions, his sleek appearance and high class line of patter always made him doubly dangerous.

The other man in the box with Nick was also familiar. He was a big, stoop-shouldered, silly-panned goon tagged Georgie Bister. He was Nick's errand boy, trigger man and general housekeeper. Bister looked like a furry-eared St. Bernard, adoring his master with red-rimmed, patient eyes.

I was still wondering why those two first citizens of the underworld were staked out in the box like honest taxpayers when the lights went down, the conductor's baton up and, in a blare of brass, the entertainment got under way.

Libby Hart had put me in the know about its star. Suzette Darcy was the latest sensation on the silver blades. An unknown Minnesota rink habitué one scant year ago, Suzy had suddenly burst into prominence. Like a shooting star she appeared in the heavens of the amusement world, challenging Sonja Henie and all the other performers who had found there was a fortune in ice—if you cut it with skates and not with an ax.

Lib had hinted that there was plenty of coin behind Suzette. The minute she made her appearance I understood why. The gal was gorgeous!

Young, beautiful, with a figure more curved than the 8's she clicked off, her gleaming, copper-colored hair, long and unbound, whirled in the breeze she stirred up. I was close enough to see her eyes were a dusky, shining blue and her mouth a tempting crimson patch.

Her charm and beauty landed with solid impact on the customers. She hadn't been in public view for more than two minutes before any *Variety* scout understood that both she and the ice show were due to be a tremendous hit and a financial fireball.

You could feel it in the air.

"What do you do next?" I asked the girl friend when intermission came along.

"I have an appointment with Miss Darcy after the performance," Libby murmured. She patted her bag. "Contracts are right here, ready for her signature, together with a certified check. How come you never learned to skate, Johnny?"

"Where I came from," I told her, "we used water for drinking purposes only."

Libby wrinkled her cute little ski-jump nose and consulted her program. I looked in the direction of the Messrs. Caduro and Bister. The perfectly groomed gunny was stifling a polite yawn. The sloppy rum-dumb beside him was scratching an ear and contemplating the wealthy Amos Tinsley with a dreamy, retrospective gaze.

Finally it was over. The crowd stood and cheered for five minutes. The fascinating Suzette made many bows. Then the lights came up and we joined the mob pushing a way out.

"Miss Darcy told me to give her a half hour," Lib murmured. "Notice what time it is now, Johnny."

It was eleven-thirty on the dot. To get rid of the half hour I took Mrs. Hart's only daughter across to a java joint and bought two cups of the Brazilian brew. As we went in I saw Lieutenant Larry Hartley, of the Homicide Division, at the end of the counter. Larry was dunking a doughnut. He glanced up, smiled at Libby and nodded at me.

"Hello, Castle. Been over at the ice cube festival? Sharp show, eh?"

Hartley wasn't a bad sort. On and off, for some time, I'd been tossed in with him on certain murderous matters that had occasionally cropped up. I liked Hartley more than I did his superior in the department, Captain Fred Mullin, a bulldog technician who growled like a man.

"Wasn't that your policeman friend?" Lib inquired, as we found a booth and edged in.

"One of them. But don't be alarmed. I have nothing in common with the Lieutenant."

LIBBY'S liquid dark eyes glinted. She drew a little breath.

"You'd better not have! You promised me you were through with crime. Remember?"

To get to the dressing rooms at the Paladium, we had to go down the block and around the corner. Every cab doing business in mirthful Manhattan had converged on the place. They mingled with chauffeur-driven, six-grand limousines and fifteen-year-old fall-aparts that only the auto shortage kept out of the junk pile.

The Paladium's stage door was ganged up with a horde of well-wishers, the curious, bobby-sox autograph addicts and delivery boys from the bigger and better flower shops.

Replacing the legendary doorman, of suspenders and sour disposition, was an impressive, uniform wearing party who listened to Libby before examining her credentials. He went into conference with a backstage board of directors and they finally decided to pass us in.

"Third floor," he said. "Take the elevator down the corridor."

We did, getting out on an overhanging cement tier patterned with doors. The lighting was indirect. Small sofas and chairs, for the comfort and convenience of visitors, were scattered along the way. It was luxuriously different from the backstage world of the ordinary side-street playhouse.

The layout was de luxe, from the shining chromium knobs on the stainless steel doors to the clubroom atmosphere pervading the place.

Suzette Darcy's dressing room was at the end of the tier, near a flight of fire-exit stairs. No one could miss it. The star's name was gold-leafed neatly over a pearl bell button. Libby put a gloved thumb on that.

I said, "Don't ring; the door is open."

She pressed the button anyway, giving me a quizzical stare.

"Stop drooling, Johnny. And remember this—when I introduce you, look, don't touch!"

"Yes, ma'am. But do you think she's in?"

Libby rang again—and again. Then she began to frown, drawing a set of arched brows together and pursing her lips.

"Wait here," she said finally. "I'll go in. If she's decent, I'll call you."

No more than two or three minutes elapsed. During it I listened to a murmur of voices coming out of the rooms on the tiers below. Gay, happy voices. Excited voices belonging to the members of the troupe. Overjoyed voices, because the show was in the bag for a protracted New York stay.

Suddenly I heard something else.

That came as a muffled, strangled scream from the doorway Libby had gone through!

I had it open in a flash and darted inside. Electric lights dazzled me for an instant. Mirrors on nearly all the walls reflected my image, but I didn't stop for any self admiration.

There were two dames stretched out on the deeply rugged floor of the dressing room. One was Libby Hart and a glance was enough to show me she had fainted.

With the other gal it was different.

Suzette Darcy, still in her radiant

finale costume, lay huddled between one mirrored wall and a mahogany dressing table that looked as long as a freight car. Her complexion was white where the makeup ended. So white that the ugly, crimson stain soaking the front of the costume, and trickling down over one folded arm, was like a bright, ruby-red river in the light.

It was no faint.

A glance was enough to tell me the copper-haired skating star had done her last twirl. The Minnesota sensation had been booked for the long sleep—by a gun that had evidently used a large-sized slug. It was the kind of slumber an alarm clock had no effect on.

Suzy was dead!

CHAPTER II

WARNED

A TILED bath was a step off the dressing room. That boasted an icewater spigot and glasses. With a hand that shook slightly, I filled one and snatched up a towel, slopped it in cold Croton and applied it to Libby Hart's complexion.

It worked.

She sat up, making passes and shaking the dampness out of her eyes and face.

"What happened?" she said, wonderingly. "Somebody turned off the lights and—"

Then she got Miss Darcy in focus and started to encore. I used the towel again. She stayed awake and I hoisted her up off the rug.

"We're getting out of here—at least you are, fast! No testimonials tonight. Come on, pull yourself together."

Libby shuddered and let me lead her toward the stainless steel door. She buckled slightly at the knees, but managed to keep going. When I reached the door, I put a handkerchief over its knob and pulled it open.

That gave me a perfect view into slate gray eyes that were fringed with an array of thick, dark lashes.

They belonged to a small, pretty, very blond girl who wore a short, smart broadtail jacket and no hat.

She wasn't smiling. There was grim determination on her curved, vermilion lips. She looked at Lib. Then she looked at me. Then she said:

"I beg your pardon. Do you know if Miss Darcy's busy?"

Libby choked. I tried to make it cheerful. I answered, "Miss Darcy isn't doing anything at the moment."

"In that case," the blondie said, "I'll go in. My name is Nan Tinsley."

She made a move to pass me. I put a hand on her arm. A nice, soft, rounded arm under the broadtail.

"Sorry. You'd better not—go in. Miss Darcy's just been murdered!"

The slate gray eyes went wide and dark. The curved mouth lost its fixed smile. Nan Tinsley shifted her gaze quickly to Libby. The girl friend's strained, horror-stricken expression was all Nan Tinsley needed to confirm my statement.

Before anyone could say "Police!" she had spun around on her high heels and was streaking down the cement-lined tier.

Five minutes later I put Libby Hart in a taxi, shoved a bill in the hackie's hand and supplied her home address. Libby didn't protest. She was still in a daze, still crushed and shaken.

"Cheer up, honey." I patted her hand before I closed the door. "You've just saved your company a wad of testimonial dough. I'll phone later."

The taxi chugged off and I hotfooted it back to the dressing room on the third tier.

Still using a handkerchief, to give the fingerprint boys a break, I closed the door and took a look around.

On the dressing table were a half dozen samples from Arcady House. I noticed a pound jar of cold cream in a handsomely decorated container before I glanced about in search of the gun.

There wasn't any sign of it. I combed through the dressing room and then the tiled bath. I figured the killer must have walked in, banged away, shoved the smoker in his clothes and walked out. Then I remembered the difficulty Libby and I had had getting past the stage doorman. At the same minute I recalled the fire-exit stairway, a couple of strides from the dressing room door.

It was no trick for anyone to have come up them for target practise and left by the same way.

I went back and looked at the dead girl. The folded back arm caught and held my attention. The hand, graceful and white, was half turned over and half open. Its palm glistened oddly. Swallowing, I leaned to get a better look.

After that I used the telephone in the corner of the room for two calls. One to the City Desk at the *Orbit*. The other to Headquarters.

Twenty minutes after that the dressing room was full of uniformed authority.

THE flashlight brigade, fingerprint experts, Captain Fred Mullin with his two trained yes-and-no men, Dave Wheeler and the same Larry Hartley who had been at the coffee counter. They were flanked by a stenographer, ready for statements, and a specialist from Ballistics.

I was high on Mullin's Hate Parade. It had to do with a piece I'd written for the *Orbit*. That had dealt with antiquated police routines as practised by the Captain, with the aid of long pieces of hose and thousand-watt electric light bulbs.

Mullin hadn't enjoyed my sarcasm. Like an elephant he hadn't forgotten, either. I knew he was waiting for a chance to even up.

"So you're the party who telephoned?" A pleased smile began to spread over his granite pan. "I've been waiting a long time, Castle—"

"Not for this one," I interrupted, pleasantly. "I've got an alibi that's practically foolproof."

I gave it to him on a plush lined platter. The smile faded out. Mullin barked orders and swung around on me again.

"I'm not through with you yet," he growled. "Stay put."

I sat down opposite the dressing table and chain-smoked. I watched Homicide at work. Doc Bagby, the medical examiner, was busy in a corner, using a couple of drawn together tables. Hartley and Wheeler hunted for the gun. The fingerprint gang threw powder around and the photographers exploded flashlights.

While that was going on, I did some thinking. Suzette had been on the stage at eleven-thirty. At midnight she was dead. In those thirty minutes she had gone back to the dressing room, but she hadn't had time to peel her costume off or get into a robe.

The killer could have been waiting for her, either parked in the bath or in full view. He hadn't lost much time. He must have blasted her fast and left in a hurry.

Why?

What had he come for? What was his motive? Why should anyone want to knock off a dame as charming and beautiful as Suzette Darcy?

Mullin consulted with his entourage and came back to me.

"Where's the gun, Castle?" he snapped.

"What gun?"

"The one you must have found while you were moseying into my business—here."

"No rod, Captain. Not even one you could hang a curtain on." I got up. "Have a frisk—free."

The fishy eyes drilled into me. Mullin didn't accept the invitation. Instead he put a big hand between my shoulders and pushed.

"Go on, get out of here! The more I look at you, the less I want to see of you!"

"That's an even money bet," I said, putting on my hat. "In my book the feeling's pari-mutuel!"

Instead of taking the elevator down, I opened the door shielding the fire-exit stairs. I wanted to see where they went. Dim lights burned on each landing. On the ground floor the door opening out was locked.

From its location I figured it led to the side street. Back, up a flight, I headed toward the stage door, passing dressing rooms now empty and silent.

The squad cars had put a group of the morbidly curious outside the Paladium's performers' entrance. I went through the crowd, turning west toward Broadway.

Half a block and I had the feeling I was being tailed. Someone had pulled away from the knot at the stage door and was ambling after me. I slowed down until he walked under an arc light.

I had a view of a big, stoop-shouldered, slow moving guy, familiar from the dented-in crown of his dicer to the baggy ends of his trousers.

He was Georgie Bister, Nick Caduro's jack-of-all-trades.

I braked at the corner, waiting for Bister to come up. The move evidently disconcerted him. He was grinning sheepishly when he reached me.

"Hello, Castle. Nice night, ain't it?"

"Why the tail?"

BISTER threw away the match stick he'd been munching on. "Tail?" As if just remembering, he said, "Look, Castle. Nick asked me to give you a message in case I saw you. He wants you to drop around to his place for a drink."

"Tell him thanks. I'm on the wagon."

That didn't do. Bister shook his head slowly. "Look, Castle. I don't want no trouble. I hate trouble. Nick said, when I saw you, I should bring you up to his flat."

"And if I don't want to go?"

Georgie patted his pocket significantly. "I guess you'll go, Castle."

He stopped a cab, held the door open for me to get in and in less than fifteen minutes we were on Central Park West. The meter-cheater pulled up in front of a massive brick building called the Stanwich Arms. Bister followed me into an elevator and out of it on the fifteenth floor.

We went down a hall and to a door. Georgie rang the bell and Nick Caduro answered it.

"Why, it's Castle. Come in." He held the door wider.

The shiny haired bad man had taken off dinner coat and vest. The glossy white of his dress shirt accented his swarthy complexion. He led the way into a living room where some inferior decorator had been allowed to run loose and waved me into a chair.

"What's the idea, Nick?" I tried to make it sound indignant, but I was worried. I didn't like early morning calls on characters of Caduro's type.

He told Bister to shake up some alcohol and hooked his thumbs in the black silk of the suspenders holding up his high-waisted pants.

"I hear how the babe who laid 'em in the aisles at the Paladium got herself shot up," Caduro continued, his tone quietly conversational. "Too bad. Friend of hers, Castle?"

"I never saw her until tonight."

"But you called on her in her dressing room. Georgie saw you and your doll at the stage door. He heard who you were asking for. You came out and put your gal in a taxi. Then you went back. You were there a long time before the badges arrived. Right?"

"Georgie has twenty-twenty vision. So what?"

"So you'd better get up and let him check on what you've got in your pockets," Nick purred.

"A hold-up?"

"No, not exactly. Just a look-over."

Bister came away from a portable mahogany bar and waited for me to get out of the chair. He had opened his spotted topcoat. He licked his lips, said, "Hold your arms up and out. This won't take long," and began to feel through my pockets.

Caduro's order for the feel around had an angle. As he said, I'd been in Suzette Darcy's dressing room. He knew it. Bister was frisking me to find out if I'd found anything there and had brought it away with me.

Anything, I thought, such as a murder gun, for instance. Or, possibly, some overlooked bit of evidence not turned in to Mullin.

Georgie made it complete. He checked my belt to see if it were the money-carrying kind. He even ran his fingers over the cuffs of my trousers. I took off my shoes at his request and he examined the interiors and heels.

Finally Bister straightened up. He shook his head.

"Clean Nick."

It was impossible to tell from Caduro's basilisk stare whether he was disappointed or not. His thin smile still displayed his square, white teeth.

He said, "Sit down, Castle. Have a drink."

"I don't use the stuff. Besides, I'm overdue on a date—with a single bed. If you don't mind I'll be running along. Nice to have seen you."

For a minute the smile faded. His glinting eyes narrowed slightly. He shrugged and nodded.

"I'll see you out." We walked to the foyer, Bister peering after us. "By the way, if I were you, I wouldn't nose around with this Paladium thing too much, Castle. I like the way you write for the *Orbit*. I'd hate to be reading some new guy's stuff."

He stopped at the hall door and slid a cigarette between his lips. I didn't say anything. Caduro began to smile again.

"Another thing. I wouldn't mention the fact you stopped in here tonight, either. To anyone." He opened the door, stepping aside to let me pass.

"Because," he added, softly, "you never know when you might get an attack of dropsy—and fall right out of circulation!"

CHAPTER III

GOLD SUITE

NEXT morning the front pages of the metropolitan press headlined the mysterious killing of the coppery-haired Suzette Darcy. Bill Jamison, the *Orbit's* top crime narrator, had turned in his usual well done job on the dressing room smear.

I read it over a quick cup of coffee in a cafeteria across from the Winter Garden. According to Bill, Mullin's score on his preliminary investigation had been a hundred percent zero. Homicide had been busy interviewing people and trying to find suspects, with no results. The Darcy murder had all the earmarks of being the unsolved crime of the year.

When I got down to the office, Jamison, tired from his all night leg work, was at his desk. He wore a green eyeshade and a frayed look. He stopped tapping the typewriter when I dropped down on the edge of his desk and grinned.

"They tell me you found the body, Johnny. You didn't run across a motive at the same time?"

"No. What's your opinion?"

Jamison shrugged. "Could be anything. Love affair that went wrong, private blackmail — the usual, that brings on sudden death. I learned one interesting thing. Do you know whose dough backed the skating show?"

I stretched for an answer. "Tinsley?"

Bill pushed up his eyeshade. "Right. How did you learn that?"

"Just a guess. I saw him there last night. Tinsley's a Minnesota taxpayer. Suzy came from there. I don't know how I happened to make the link. What about Tinsley?"

Jamison looked at his shorthand notes. "He's been a widower for ten years. He's worth twenty million. He's the party who bought the Emory Emeralds, as they're called, from some Indian potentate and gave them to his late wife. Six perfect green stones, each worth a flock of coin."

Jamison added: "Mrs. Tinsley's jewel collection was second to none in this country. The emeralds, done up in the form of a short necklace, were the top item. I dug that out of the files in the morgue at four o'clock this morning, Johnny."

"Where would Nick Caduro fit in?" I asked, after a long pause.

"Caduro? That punk!" Bill took off the eyeshade. "You don't mean he's in on this?"

"Nickie boy was over at the ice frolic last night. Nick knew all about me being in the Darcy dressing room. He was so interested, he sent his triggerman, Georgie Bister, up to invite me up to his apartment at the Stanwich Arms for a drink. After Bister frisked me, Caduro gave me a red light. He told me I was due for lead poisoning if I mentioned my call."

Jamison's eyes began to gleam. "Caduro, eh? Thanks for the tip, Johnny. If that mug is interested, it might mean plenty."

"Keep me out of it," I said. "I like breathing!" As an afterthought, I asked: "By the way, where does Tinsley hole in?"

"Hotel Republic," Bill answered. "He's got the Gold Suite there. Why? You're not thinking of stopping in to see him?"

"No—not him."

I called Libby at Arcady House. She

was at her desk and not overjoyed with the way I had gotten rid of her the previous night. I made a dinner date and glanced at my watch. It was a few minutes after eleven—a good time for a pre-lunch call.

The Hotel Republic, midway up aristocratic Park Avenue, boasted a lobby that looked like a Hollywood movie set. In technicolor. I had to wait around while telephone calls announcing my presence were being relayed back and forth.

Finally one of the desk clerks, a wistful-eyed party in a cutaway coat, informed me I could use one of the elevators.

The Gold Suite did business on the twentieth story. A male servant with the same droopy eyes as his boss ushered me into a lounge room with a view. I was taking a cut of it when, some five minutes later, the door opened and Nan Tinsley entered.

The little blondie was wearing a dragon-embroidered Chinese housecoat in place of the broadtail jacket. Bare feet were in silver sandals. In the morning sunshine her gold hair glimmered like the stuff at Fort Knox.

SHE looked at me and I saw recognition in the slate gray eyes.

"Oh!" she said.

"Sit down, Miss Tinsley. I'll make this brief. I stopped around to ask you a few routine questions."

"Are you with the police? Mr. Darbill, the clerk downstairs, said you were a newspaper reporter who wanted an interview."

"That's right. But my interest in Miss Darcy's murder has a police connection. I'm trying to turn up some clues I can hand Homicide, thus helping them and the paper I work for."

"What do you want to ask me?" I sensed rather than saw her begin to chill.

"You went to see Miss Darcy last night. Why? What about?"

"That was a personal matter." Her tone was suddenly defensive.

"Don't let's beat bushes, Miss Tinsley," I said. "Murder's murder and nothing's personal when investigations get underway. Be frank with me and I'll save you a lot of assorted headaches."

"I don't understand," she said.

"The Police would like to know why you went to see Suzette Darcy last night. They usually like to know everything about everybody. If I mentioned your call, Captain Mullin of Homicide would want you at Headquarters for some chitchat. Mullin is a very coarse, unsympathetic individual. Not your type at all. And, naturally, there'd be a lot of newspaper reporters with their ears hanging out. The minute you appeared, they'd have you all over the front pages of their papers—with pictures. You know, 'Millionaire's Heiress Tied In With Paladium Pass-out'."

The slate gray eyes darkened. The blondie's slender, red-tipped fingers began to move up and down along the sash of the Chinese housecoat. She helped herself to a cigarette from a crystal container, took a drag on it and looked at me thoughtfully.

"There's no mystery about it," she said, finally. "I've known Miss Darcy for quite a while. She came from a town near where I live in Minnesota. I merely wanted to congratulate her."

She made it sound authentic, but some sixth sense told me there was more to it than that. I looked at her quizzically. She began to smile. A pleasant, red-lipped little smile that said, "Kick that around. What are you going to do about it?"

I got up. It looked like a blank—until I reached the doors. The sad faced servant who had let me in opened them suddenly and coughed.

"Begging your pardon, Miss Nan. There's a telephone call for you. Will you take it in here?"

"Phone call?" The little blond mashed out her cigarette.

"Mr. Caduro is on the wire, Miss Nan."

I bowed out, something tingling from the end of my spine to the top of my scalp. Caduro! Nickie telephoning Amos Tinsley's daughter! All of a sudden I began to understand how far in on the tangle the patent-leather-haired hooligan was.

Through the lobby and out to the street. I was under the Republic's bronze canopy when Larry Hartley, cutting in from the curb, started up the steps.

The Lieutenant gave me a glance sharp enough to shave with.

"I've been looking for you, Castle. The Captain wants to split some more conversation with you—concerning last night. I'll only be a minute here. Wait!"

Hartley went through the revolving door. He was gone five minutes. He came back, his face expressionless.

"Okay, Johnny. Let's go."

Captain Mullin was in one of his moody humors. I saw that when I sat down in his office. That meant Mullin, instead of employing his usual hillbully tactics, would try to be cute and clever. On him it wasn't becoming.

"So you were pegged coming out of the Hotel Republic," Mullin began, when Hartley told him where he had found me. "Out of your territory, isn't it? What were you doing up there?"

I answered, "I'll have to see a mouthpiece before I answer questions. Or am I under arrest?"

"You will be if you don't stop trying to be foxy with me. I'll tell you why you were there. You went up to see Amos Tinsley."

THE Captain unloaded that with gestures. He looked as smug as a rabbit that had just pulled a magician out of a hat.

"Incorrect, Captain. Go to the foot of the class."

"Tinsley wasn't in," Hartley murmured, over Mullin's lumpy shoulders. "I telephoned up to find out."

The head of Homicide fastened his fishy eyes on me. He put one half-soled eleven on the slide of his desk and tried to look tough. That didn't require much effort.

"I'm warning you, Castle. You're attempting to solve the Paladium thing on your own. I know how you operate. You want a scoop for your paper and the heck with the New York Police Department."

I didn't say anything. Hartley looked out the window. Mullin cleared his throat and continued:

"It's your duty as a citizen to turn any evidence you have over to me. I let you loose last night, thinking maybe you'd co-operate. I see now it's the same old stuff. You're playing solo and trying to make a monkey out of me."

It was on the tip of my tongue to tell him nature had beaten me to it. But I didn't. Instead, I gave him one of my friendliest smiles and shrugged.

"I don't know what you're talking about, Captain. It's all Greek to me."

"What did you want to see Amos Tinsley about? How did you know he was a friend of Suzette Darcy's? Who gave you the slant on that?"

My ears went up. So the ex-Flour King was a friend of the dead Suzy? Stick around Headquarters, I thought, and you learn things.

"That's no secret," I said. "It's public news that Tinsley backed the ice show. Or isn't it?"

The telephone rang and Mullin reached for it. Before he picked it up he growled:

"You don't want to do business with me? You're lone-wolfing it. All right, Castle. I warned you to lay off. Don't, and see what happens to you! That's all for now."

I got up. "Drop over to my place some night soon." I invited.

"What for?" Mullin grunted.

"We'll open a gas jet!" I said—and left fast.

CHAPTER IV

Information

WHILE riding uptown in a cab, I was thinking hard.

What the icicle-eyed Captain had let out of the bag concerning the ex-Flour King of St. Paul and his friendship with the glamorous Suzette, had started a train of thought that gathered speed at every whistle-stop.

I had a double choice.

One, to try and see Tinsley and in some way dig information out of him. The kind it was likely Mullin *hadn't* gotten. The other angle was Tinsley's attractive daughter.

The first score had been all in her favor. But I had a stronger in now.

The Caduro tie-up seemed to be as good as three kings and a pair of aces.

At the end of Longacre I let the cab go and found an empty telephone booth in a corner drugstore. My nickel gave me the voice of the old servant who had admitted me to the Gold Suite earlier that morning. He said Mr. Tinsley was out. He didn't know what time he'd be back.

"Let me talk to Miss Tinsley," I said.

"I'm sorry, sir. She isn't at home, either."

"You wouldn't know where she went? This," I lied, smoothly, "is an old family friend from St. Paul."

"Which?" The voice in my ear dripped honey.

I remembered he had probably been with the Tinsleys for years and knew all their pals. So I slipped the receiver back on the hook and went down to the newspaper.

Jamison's desk was vacant. There was a load of mail on mine, mostly from fight managers, seeking free publicity for aspiring hopefuls. I sorted through it, pushed it aside and thought hard.

I was still trying to find the answer when I saw Jamison come in. He reached his desk the same time I did.

"Break?"

Bill shook his head. "What's the matter with that cement-head called Mullin? All of a sudden he changes his mind. It's minimum coverage from now on. For security reasons, he says. I can't even learn if he's got the gun. It's a blank wall."

Jamison lighted a cigarette and slumped down in his chair.

"I've got an angle," I said slowly. "I don't know how to play it. Tinsley's daughter knows something, but won't spill. I saw her after I left here this morning. Somebody was telephoning her when she handed me my hat. The name was Caduro!"

Jamison's head snapped up with a jerk. "You're kidding!"

"I'm leveling. What can Miss Tinsley have in common with that bandit? And how can I get to see her again and put on the clamp? I'm sure I can shake a lot of valuable talk loose if I can get her vocabulary started. How?"

"That's easy," Jamison said. "Hang around the Republic's lobby until she comes in or goes out."

"She's out now and she might not get back until the wee small hours." I shook my head. "No good."

"Why don't you get Beth to phone her? Maybe the butler's suspicious of a masculine voice. Maybe he has his orders."

"It's a notion," I said, and went out to the switchboard.

Beth Wheaton, one of the plug swingers who sailed from Brooklyn and got most of her comedy via the radio, glanced up when I parked.

"Oh, Mr. Castle, in the flesh. You're wishing a number, maybe?" Dialect went with the question.

"How would you like to earn a five spot?"

"Make it dollars instead of spots and I'll say yes. You want me to call your girl friend and tell her you're working late tonight?"

"I want you to call up the Hotel Republic and talk about Miss Nan Tinsley."

"Oh, society stuff, he asks for." I took a bill out of my leather and let her glom its denomination. "Okay, Mr. Castle. What do I say and how do I say it?"

I gave her a quick briefing and—waited.

The Brooklyn accent wasn't too good, but the droopy-eyed servant evidently wasn't suspicious. Beth rattled it off as instructed, thanked him and pulled the plug out.

"Miss Tinsley," she said, "is at the matinee at the Fine Arts Theayter. She's not returning for dinner. Lucky dame!"

THE playhouse had a quarter to five curtain. I was propped in the lobby fifteen minutes before the audience came out. The show was heavy, drawing-room drama. It had knocked off fourteen consecutive weeks and looked good for a summer run.

Finally the lobby doors were pinned back and the patrons began to come through. They were nearly all out before I had a glimpse of the one I waited for.

Nan Tinsley, alone, and in a completely different outfit from the one she had featured at the Paladium, slipped across the tiles and was bee-lining for a taxi when I went after her.

The taxi stopped and she got in. So did I.

I pulled the door shut and said, "Riverside Drive. I'll tell you when to stop," to the hackie. Then I turned and looked into gray eyes full of sparks.

"What's the meaning of this?" Nan Tinsley demanded, frost hanging on every word.

"Plenty. You held out this morning. I gave you an even break and you tried to cheat. This time it's going to be different."

"Yes?" The sparks burned out, but her pretty face still remained as informative as a piece of stone.

"I've learned a couple of things. About your father being friendly with Suzette Darcy. So far that's been under the counter. The police haven't released it. I'll have to if you don't open up."

She drew her red underlip between her teeth. I made sure the glass partition between the front and back of the cab was shut. I breathed in the smell of white lilacs. It came from the green dress Nan Tinsley was wearing under her new look coat.

"Turn this taxi around and take me back to the hotel!" There was a snap in her voice. "I have a dinner date!"

"With Nick Caduro?"

She didn't answer for a minute. She didn't have to. From the wondering light that flashed in her eyes I knew I had scored.

"You can turn around," I said to the driver, pushing the partition open. "Take us down to Centre Street, Police Headquarters."

The hackie gave me a fast glance, nodded and turned the ark at the first corner going the right way. Nan Tinsley drew further back on the worn upholstery. Her mouth was a red, stubborn line. Her gloved fingers wove together and the perfume of lilacs increased.

I waited.

Five blocks. Then ten. The taxi kept going and she kept quiet. I figured she was obstinate enough to ride the whole way when she suddenly cracked.

"You're not really going to take me to the police? You're trying to bulldoze me?" Her tone had a tremor.

It was my turn to keep quiet.

"What do you want to know?" She asked it abruptly, a catch in her voice.

"Pull around the next street and take us uptown again." I directed the driver. He gave me another swift look and touched his cap. I shoved the partition shut and turned to the blond. "What did you go up to Suzette Darcy's dressing room for? And don't say congratulations or autograph."

It took a long time coming. Nan Tinsley wasn't the kind who folded fast. She was still trying to see her way out.

Finally she drew a deep breath and straightened.

"My father was at Headquarters this morning. He must have told them about the emeralds. If they know it, everyone else will—sooner or later. I wanted to ask Suzette to return them. That's the reason I went to see her last night."

I let her talk on.

"The Emory Emeralds belonged to my mother. Maybe you've heard of them. They're very famous and worth a lot of money. My father had no right to give them to Suzette. They really belong to me—my mother wanted me to have them! Dad knows that, but—but—"

"Your father thought they'd go good with copper hair?" I put in.

SHE was started now, and she answered my question without hesitation.

"It isn't entirely his fault!" She drew another breath. "From what I know, Miss Darcy had been working on him ever since she first saw the emeralds. And Dad—well, he's not as young as he once was and I suppose he was flattered by her attention. You know how men get. He did anything she asked—anything and everything. I didn't care about the money he spent. But when he started giving her something that belongs to me, I thought it was time to call a halt."

"The cops could get you a Grand Jury indictment on that one statement!" I murmured.

"I didn't kill her!" The gray eyes flashed again. "All I wanted to do was see her. She was carefully avoiding me. I wanted to tell her she couldn't keep the emeralds. That they weren't my father's to give! That's why I went to her dressing room last night."

It added up. I thought fast. An old man's infatuation for a glamorous gal who was on the make and take. This motive was one hundred percent sound. The emeralds had been green lights to Death!

"What about Nick Caduro? Where does he come in?"

Nan Tinsley's curved lips tightened. The stubborn look froze her face again. But I knew the system now. When she shifted her gaze, I made a show of reaching out to push the partition back.

That did it.

"Mr. Caduro's a private detective I hired the other day."

It was my turn to stare. I wanted to laugh, but I didn't. It wasn't a gag with her. Her tone was as serious as a major operation.

"Private detective? How did you meet him? What did you hire him for?"

She pressed her fingers together. "At first I thought I should have help to get the emeralds back. I didn't know what Suzette would do. If she refused to return them, I decided to have them taken away from her. I don't know much about police methods, but I had an idea a private detective was what I needed. So I engaged Mr. Caduro's services."

"Where did you find him?" I was really interested.

"I don't mind telling you. I was in the cocktail lounge at the hotel. It was last Tuesday, about five o'clock. The house detective stopped at my table for a minute. I knew him because father had given him a big tip for finding a suitcase Hutchins had misplaced when we checked in. Hutchins is the one who admitted you this morning."

"I remember. Go on. What did you say to the house detective?"

"I asked him if he could recommend a private detective agency. He gave me two or three names. He wrote them down on the back of the wine card. Then he went away. He hadn't been gone more than a minute or two before Mr. Caduro, who had been seated nearby, got up and came over."

I nodded. "Nickie boy had overheard your conversation. Opportunity never has to knock twice for him. So he told you he was a private detective and would be glad to offer his services. What did he do for credentials and an office address?"

Nan Tinsley said that the white-toothed Caduro had shown her a badge and explained that, due to renting conditions, his office was waiting to be opened. Meanwhile, he was operating directly from his suite at the Stanwich Arms. I could imagine the oily line he had tossed her, the suave, convincing way he had worked himself into her confidence.

"And," I said, out loud, "you hired him and told him about the Emory Emeralds. What did he say?"

"That he'd get them back for me. All he wanted was five hundred dollars as a retainer."

My mind clicked like the meter on the cab. Light began to shine through. Caduro, in the role of a private eye! A fortune in emeralds dished up and handed him! The kind of a grab that comes once in a lifetime! Custom-made and built to size!

No wonder, I told myself, the sloppy Bister had given me the frisk in Nick's rooms. That was more than sufficient. It showed me that Caduro hadn't gotten the green gems. He had an idea I might have picked it up and that fact brought a swarm of ideas and questions buzzing through my brain.

Someone had murdered Suzette Darcy for the Emory Emeralds, but hadn't been able to fetch them away. Something, somewhere, had gone wrong. They'd put on the kill, but had failed to collect. The finger of suspicion leveled at Caduro. He knew about the famous jewels. Yet, if his gun had hurled the slug into the ice star, there hadn't been a payoff—yet.

"Can I go back to the hotel now?"

Nan Tinsley's voice had a quaver again. I said, "Sure," and gave the chauffeur the Hotel Republic as a new address. Then I added:

"But you're not keeping any engagement with Mr. Caduro—if you have one—tonight. I'm introducing you to a feminine friend of mine, a Miss Hart. I'll see that she keeps you out of trouble."

Nan Tinsley's brows went up. "What kind—" she began, stopping when I clipped it off short and said:

"Private eye trouble! In the fashionable raiment of Nick Caduro."

Then I explained, while the taxi rolled toward Park Avenue and the hotel.

CHAPTER V

Fancy Shooting

MY WATCH showed it was almost seven o'clock when I got back to my rooms. They were in the shadow of the Winter Garden. At one time the building had been a livery stable. Some smart operator, realizing each stall would make a three room suite, had done some remodeling. The agent who had rented me the place said it was lucky.

There was a horseshoe in every room.

The minute I unlocked the front door I realized I'd had visitors. The place looked as if a junior cyclone had hit it. Someone had given it a complete going over, not missing a thing on the way.

The drawers in all the furniture had been emptied on the floor. The mattress had been slashed and pulled apart. Feathers from the pillows lay like snowflakes in the bedroom. Even the pictures on the walls had been dragged down.

I looked at the wreckage. Bister? It was the sloppy type of job a sloppy guy like Georgie would do.

So the neat Nick still thought I had the green flash? That was reassuring in one degree. It meant that Caduro would stick around for awhile longer. And I needed time to do some headwork on an angle and an idea that had popped into my mind after I had gotten Libby on the phone and blarneyed her into playing chaperon for the blond Miss Tinsley that evening.

Lib hadn't liked any part of it. Starting with the canceled dinner date, and having a sneaking suspicion I was up to my old tricks again, it had required a lot of soft talk and hard logic to get her to agree to my plan.

I put out the lights and left the mess as was. It wasn't hard to figure how my visitor had gotten in. Any kind of a key worked on the front door. I'd never bothered to put a burglar-proof lock on it. All that would have done would have been to send uninvited callers around to the rear windows. They were a mere five feet from the areaway.

When I went out I cased the block. When Mullin thought I was chiseling, he had a habit of sticking a shag on me. It was likely, also, that the unconvinced Caduro might have Georgie hidden out somewhere nearby to watch.

But nobody tailed me to Broadway and the cafeteria where I had some quick cuisine.

The case of the murdered skating sensation was going around in circles. The same kind of dizzy whirligigs Suzette had cut on the ice of the Paladium stage. Only one thing was definite. The Emory Emeralds were still missing.

I doubted that Amos Tinsley had mentioned them to Homicide. After all, a person like the former Flour King had some pride. And the fact that Hartley had gone back to the Hotel Republic, probably for more questioning, might or might not confirm the notion that Tinsley had kept quiet about the emeralds.

What I had in mind was a long chance. I hadn't forgotten the graceful, folded back white hand of Suzette Darcy. The hand I looked at when I had first seen her crumpled figure on the dressing room floor. The recollection of it came back, swiftly and sharply, when I pondered the puzzle.

It was a hundred-to-one bet, but sometimes long shots upset the dope and breeze in.

I paid my check and started toward Columbus Circle.

Fifteen minutes later I was at the Paladium. The big amusement center, due to murder, had been closed, shut up until a new star could be found for the ice pageant. The huge building was in complete darkness.

Passing the gay posters, bright with lithographed pictures of Suzette Darcy, in exotic poses, I went on past the main gates and around the corner to the stage entrance. It was hard to believe that so few hours previous the place had been the scene of excitement and confusion. I thought of the quantity of flowers that had been delivered. Maybe they had been an omen, a bad one.

I figured the place had a watchman. The outer doors were open, the inner locked. A dim night light burned in a cement floored and walled recess. An elderly man, in a tilted back chair, slapped his feet on the cement and sat up when I walked in on him.

"Police business." I made it short and authoritative, giving him a flash at my police card.

I PUT the card away and slid a bill out of my hip pocket wallet. That interested him more. He got up, looking from the money to me and then back to the cash again.

"About last night?" he asked. When I nodded he said, "There's nobody around now. They took the cop off this afternoon."

I handed the money over. "I've got to go up for awhile. Okay?"

"Sure, help yourself. I'm making my rounds now. Take all the time you want."

He shoved the bill into his pocket and unlocked the inside doors. Then he pulled a switch and more of the small, wan lights flickered on inside.

The elevators weren't running, but that didn't make much difference. I found the stairs and went up to the third tier. My footsteps made hollow echoes as I walked along. The quiet came back to me, eerily. The stainless steel door of the star's dressing room was shut but unlocked.

This time I didn't use a handkerchief to open it. I felt around inside until I found the wall switch. That turned on the current in a couple of lamps and filled the mirror walls with my reflection.

Except that the dressing room had been cleaned up of exploded flash bulbs, cigar ashes and fingerprint powder, everything was the same as it had been when I had charged in after hearing Libby's anguished scream. I glanced over at the floor where Suzy had reposed, the ominous red trickle splashing her arm and costume. There was still a stain of blood on the rug there.

My gaze shifted. It went to the dressing table, the Arcady House products, past them and to the door of the adjoining tiled bath. I moved slowly over to that. As I reached it I felt a cool current of air on my ankles.

That followed the almost soundless click of the door's latch!

Turning, I looked into the round, black O of a .45 caliber Colt automatic. That was gripped in the right hand of Nick Caduro. It was leveled at my heart line and steady as a rock.

Behind the dapper Nickie, Georgie Bister, a match stuck in one corner of his seamy-lipped mouth, stood with his back to the stainless steel, watching and enjoying every minute of it.

"Don't say I didn't warn you, Castle," Caduro said. "Remember?"

I nodded. "Yes."

"Sit down. Before I give the shooter a workout, I want a little conversation with you."

I dropped down in the same chair I'd warmed while waiting for Homicide the previous night. Carduro lowered the gun to a new level. The match in Bister's mouth changed corners.

"What have you got to say, Castle?" His tone was like the steel he held.

A chill that started at my scalp this time worked down—all the way to my shoes. I felt an inner cramp, quick and twisting. Caduro's eyes were as deadly as the weapon he gripped.

I was in for a bad session.

"You could have asked me to show George around the premises," I began, trying to keep my voice steady. "He didn't have to pull my place to pieces."

Bister laughed. Caduro snapped, "So you got to the Tinsley dame and stalled her on me? She broke the date I had with her and I don't need a blueprint to tell me why." He took a step closer, a muscle in his cheek twitching. "Let that ride. You know what I want!"

"Sure, emeralds. The Emory Emeralds. But what makes you think I have them? I was clean when Georgie went through me in your apartment. They weren't in mine. So that's that."

Caduro's lips folded back in a thin, dangerous smile.

"Sure. You were clean on two counts. But you're not clean now. What did you came back here for tonight? I'll tell you. You found the emeralds last night. You were too smart to walk out with them then. So you stashed them in here somewhere. Where?"

Bister moved away from the door. His right hand dropped carelessly in the pocket of his overcoat. The match stick stopped bobbing and weaving.

CADURO'S eyes peered at me. The cold chill spread, wrapping around me like an icy blanket.

"If the emeralds were here when the Darcy girl was bumped," I heard myself saying, "why weren't they picked up then?"

"Because," Caduro rasped, "Bister's a mouse! The gal screamed and he got scared! So scared his gun went off—this gun!"

"That's right," the rum-dumb mumbled. "Why didn't she keep her mouth shut? She wouldn't have got hurt. All I come for—"

"Shut up, you dummy!" Caduro cut in.

"Knowing about her won't do him no good where he's going," Bister whined. "Come on, Nick. Put him away and let's get out of here. I'm worried about that watchman."

Caduro's .45 burrowed into my chest. He was so close I could feel his breath on my hair and face. There was murder in his mind.

"Last half of the last inning, Castle! Where's the stuff?"

I could almost feel his finger get set on the trigger. Something came up in my throat, a lump that I couldn't swallow. My heart slowed to a waltz time tick and then began to rhumba.

After all, I told myself, what was my life compared with some green stones? And how did I know the idea I had dreamed up was the right one? Even if I told Nickie about it, and it was correct, he certainly wasn't going to turn me loose.

I knew the murderer. And that automatically made me eligible for a top spot on the stiff list and an undertaker's attention!

"Try that big can of cold cream over there," I managed to say.

Caduro stepped back. The gun came away from me. Bister gulped. It sounded like a seal swallowing a fish.

"What's it—a rib?" Georgie laughed, deep in his throat.

"Last night, when I was up here," I squeezed the words out, painfully. "I noticed one of her hands. Something glistened on it. Cold cream. There wasn't any on her face—"

"He's got something!" Bister's exclamation rang like a bell. "The dame was standing right over there when I come in. Her hands was right near that can!"

"Get it!" Caduro's command cracked like a whip. "What are you waiting for? Bring it over here!"

The sloppy Bister went for the Arcady House container like a terrier after a rat. Another order from Nick and Georgie brought a folded towel in from the bath. He stretched that out flat on the floor.

Caduro handed him the can. "Dump it."

Bister complied, but with not too much success. The thick, white substance didn't spill easily. Georgie kept rapping the sides of the can with his big hand. That didn't help much, either.

"Reach in, you dope!" Nick snarled. "Feel around!"

Georgie did. My heart stopped its pounding when his fingers waded around in the gooey stuff and began to come up with something. The lamplight flashed on what looked like green glass when Bister used his other hand to wipe the cold cream from it.

Caduro, turning sideways, bent over to see better. The big, untidy hoodlum's breathing sounded like a calliope warming up. I didn't pay any attention to it. I had been right about the place the Emory Emeralds had been cached. I hoped I was going to be right about the impulse beating at the back of my brain.

It was then or never!

I gripped the arms of the chair and shot out of it. Nick's position made him a perfect setup for attack. Bent sideways, he was not only off balance but in such a stance that mowing him down meant he would fall on top of the crouched-over Georgie.

A carom shot, if I ever saw one!

My shoulder hit him like a bowling ball between the number two and three pins. It wasn't so much strength as swiftness and surprise. With a ripped out oath Nickie boy did what I figured. He slammed into Bister and both went down, faces to the rug.

The cold cream can rolled merrily away while I grabbed for the gun that had bounced out of Caduro's hand. It was about ten inches from the tips of my fingers. I had to work fast. I was just touching the stock of the rod when Caduro wriggled out from under me and used a knee.

It was an agonizing jolt. It made me clamp my teeth down on the groan that burst out of my throat. But I kept on reaching. I had the gun the next minute. It was off safety and ready to use!

The room danced before my eyes. I was full of pain. But I hardly felt it when I saw Caduro scramble to his feet and start to come at me. I got the gun up and pressed the trigger. The room sounded as if an artillery barrage were being laid down. I kept on pumping the gun madly, wildly, until suddenly, and without notice, the lights went out and the noise stopped.

I seemed to shoot down a chute—into a lot of waiting black coal. Only, as the radio comics Beth Wheaton listened to would have said, it didn't hurt because it was soft coal.

Soft as fleece. . . .

WHEN I came out of it I thought somebody had turned the clock back.

Because the dressing room was full of uniformed authority again. I was laid out on an upholstered settee and Hartley was busy chafing my wrists. Over his left ear I saw Mullin. The stocky figure of the Captain was across the room. The emerald necklace hung suspended from one of his stubby fingers. Somebody must have cleaned off the cream. Now it sparkled and scintillated like Cartier's front window.

I looked past Mullin. A couple of plain-clothes men were giving first aid to the Messrs. Caduro and Bister. Both had been shot, Georgie in the legs and Nickie boy in the arms. Wheeler was trying handcuffs for size and Georgie was bleeding out a full confession in a mumble-jumble of words.

"Feeling better, Johnny?" Hartley picked up the flask that had left a sting in my mouth.

"I'm okay. What happened?"

"Nothing much except that two of your six shots rang bells. Good thing for you the watchman was handy, heard the racket and came in. Looks like you decided to throw a faint or something at the wrong moment. But it's all in and on the books, now. We've got the gun, the guy who murdered Suzette Darcy and the motive!"

I SAT up and lowered my feet to the floor. That felt steady under them. Caduro threw a venomous glance at me, but I didn't pay any attention. I was more interested in Captain Fred Mullin, the smile on his granite pan and the hand he held out as he flat-footed over to me.

"Much as I hate doing it," Mullin rumbled, "I've got to hand it to you, Castle. With my help you sewed this case up to the Queen's taste. How about a lift downtown—or anywhere you want to go?"

"Thanks. All I want is a telephone and a call to the Gold Suite at the Hotel Republic," I told him. "When I get my gal friend on the wire, Captain, you can speak your piece—for me."

Mullin rubbed his chin and looked puzzled.

"Yeah? What do you want me to tell her?"

I grinned and reached for the telephone.

"What a swell guy I am—and how you did all the heavy work on this one. I didn't have a thing to do with it. Right?"

He nodded and I got the number.

●

NEXT · ISSUE

TRAMPS' CHRISTMAS EVE

A Yuletide Detective Story by JOHNSTON McCULLEY

The Artistic Touch

by

LEWIS LITTLE

As the thug jumped, the policeman's gun went off

For once, the Annual Artists' Ball showed a profit—and then it had to be pilfered!

IT WAS the maddest affair the Village had seen since the war. All the long-haired boys were there, in slacks, heavy wool shirts and bow ties. Their girl friends wore berets or page-boy haircuts, manipulated longish ebony-and-silver cigarette holders, and scuffed around in woven sandals.

This was the annual Artists' Ball, and everyone was out for a gay time. The talk was mostly of "art"—suitably diluted in clouds of Turkish cigarette smoke, gallons of dry Martinis, and the latest corner cafe gossip.

You didn't have to be a genius to attend. All you needed was a reasonably good contact in the art world—and the price of a ticket. Johnny Harris had both; but he wasn't having much of a time.

Harris, as usual, was hard at work.

He sat now in the business office of the Sherman Salon, where the affair was being held, and counted the receipts. He counted folding money, silver coins, nickels and pennies. He jotted down the totals neatly, in separate columns, and then added them up.

"Sacre bleu!" Johnny Harris exclaimed. "We show a profit!"

"No! Incredible!" Herbert Miller, chairman of the ball, sauntered in. He chewed appreciatively on his Martini olive, spat out the stone, and filled his glass from a pint pocket flask.

Miller was fat, he was in his early forties, he dressed like a walking ad for surplus war clothing, and he made twenty-five grand a year painting semi-proletarian murals for Park Avenue bars.

He affected an air of nonchalant boredom, was generally broke—but somehow could spot even an old dime on the sidewalk at a hundred yards.

"Uh—what's the nest egg, Johnny?"

"One thousand, two hundred and five dollars—and sixty-nine cents," Harris added sourly.

Miller adjusted a G. I. web belt over his bulging paunch.

"That is not right, Johnny. Even worse, it is almost illegal."

"Illegal?"

"Natürlich, mein lieber Freund." Miller had once spent two weeks in Germany. "The Art Society of Lower MacDougal Street *never* shows a profit—it isn't in the tradition, you know." He reached out a fat hand. "I'll just borrow a couple hundred and send out for more gin and Vermouth."

All five feet, four inches of Johnny Harris rose to the fray.

"Over my dead body!" he protested, and snatched the currency back.

Miller was hurt.

"I am the chairman of this shindig! Remember?"

"And you had me bonded to handle the ticket sale! Remember that?"

Miller backed out of the little office.

"You discourage me, Johnny," he said sorrowfully. "Despite all our best hopes, I'm afraid you'll never have the soul of a true master. In a word, my little man, you lack the artistic touch!"

WHICH, of course, was the unkindest cut of all.

It wasn't that Harris lacked "talent," whatever that might be. But his friends generally labeled him with an all-inclusive tag.

"You are too—uh—too formal," they would say. "You paint like a still-life photographer. Your work is not sufficiently abstract. It is too mental. You look right at your subject, not through him."

Against all this, Johnny Harris was firmly set.

"I do not paint a cow chasing a pitchfork, and call it Atomic Bomb Romance!" he would protest bitterly. "I do not paint canvas all white, and say it represents Television Without Nylon Stockings In The Year Twenty-Five-Sixty-Three B. C.! I am a normal man, and I paint normal things!"

So everybody else had a marvelous time at the Artists' Ball, and Johnny Harris wound up as the treasurer.

Harris reflected now on his unhappy lot, as he slid rubber bands around the neat little packets of currency, and put them away in a small metal cash box. He put the coins in their proper compartments too. He was just about to place the cash box in the office safe, when he heard the door open and steps coming across the threshold.

Johnny Harris turned around quickly, to catch one sharp glimpse of the intruder. It wasn't Herbert Miller, chairman of the ball. It wasn't any of their mutual Village friends.

It wasn't anybody Harris had ever seen before.

He realized that, a half hour later, as he lay on a couch with a cold towel on his forehead. The hard, sudden blackjack blow on the head had come with stunning force.

And the cash box had vanished just as quickly.

"Twelve hundred dollars!" Harris said bitterly. "For the first time in my life, I am connected with a success. Then it disappears!"

Policeman Walt Anderson barely concealed a smile. Anderson had been summoned from his beat as soon as the robbery was discovered. He was a big, husky young cop, out of the Navy three years, and he liked his work.

"You didn't recognize the thief, Mr. Harris?"

"No. I couldn't tell him from Adam."

"Well," said Anderson, "I'll arrange to have you taken to the police morgue tomorrow. We have a picture file of nearly every crook in town."

Harris frowned. "I'd hate to look at all those prints. Maybe there's a better method of identification."

They let it go at that, and Harris went home to nurse his aching head. Reluctantly he agreed to visit the police morgue—if it was necessary.

Meanwhile, over at an East Side bistro, Vince Balmer—an artist of a somewhat different sort—was kicking the gong around.

"Have another drink, honey," he told the blond cutie sitting on his knee.

"Don't mind if I do, big boy." She sipped the Scotch highball with loving care. "Gee, most of the guys buy me beer. You must've robbed a bank, or something."

Balmer grinned. "Banks aren't open at this hour, kid," he said.

He was quite satisfied with himself. The job had come off like clock-work. Balmer's pals had put him wise to the artists' ball a week before.

"Drop in and have yourself a time," they'd told him. "The tickets are only a buck and a half, and the drinks are mostly free. You might even run into a couple of uptown rich chicks."

"If I do, I'll give 'em a run for their money," he had promised.

But he'd had other ideas after he showed up at the affair. The Sherman Salon might be full of odd characters, but certainly a lot of tickets had been sold. Vince Balmer had fingered the blackjack he always kept on his person.

"I begin to smell a good deal," he'd told himself.

It hadn't been hard to find Johnny Harris' office. The stickup was even simpler. Balmer hadn't even bothered to slip a handkerchief over his face, once he'd spotted the layout.

"This'll be over before the lug can get a second look," he decided.

Yes, it had been just like that. Nobody had stopped him for so much as a second. The little metal cash box now reposed in an ash can, wiped clean of fingerprints. And its contents rested snugly in Vince Balmer's pockets.

BALMER ordered himself another Scotch and soda, bounced the blonde dish off his knee, and reached out for a brunette who had caught his fancy all of ten seconds before.

"Well, I never!" stormed the blonde, straightening her dress.

"Beat it, sister," Balmer growled.

"Take a powder, Mildred," the brunette backed him up. "You haven't got what he takes!"

Vince Balmer made out with the brunette. At least, that was his general impression when he piled into bed just before dawn. He slept very soundly, except for a dream toward the end.

The dream concerned a naked blue eye, staring stonily from a rigid white background. The eye followed him wherever he went. It never talked, it never cried, it seldom even blinked. It simply tailed him for a whole day.

That night (according to the dream) as Balmer lounged at a bar, the eye stalked into the saloon and walked right up to him. It jumped from the floor to the foot rail, from the rail to the bar, and from the bar to Balmer's shoulder.

It did a tapdance on his shoulder, while he stared at it fascinated, and then it said quite clearly and distinctly:

"Wake up, Balmer! Drag yourself out of the sack. You're wanted down at Headquarters."

Balmer sat up slowly, shaking his head, got one bloodshot eye open, and saw a policeman standing at the side of the bed.

"Who are you?"

"I'm the truant officer," announced Officer Walt Anderson. "You're late for school, Vince. Snap it up, mug! Climb into your pants and let's get going."

Balmer sank back against the pillow, groaning sleepily.

"Beat it, junior. Ya got a search warrant?"

"Nope. I don't need one."

Balmer yawned heavily. "You cops got nothing on me. You been tryin' to pin a rap on me for the last year. I got witnesses that can vouch for me every night this week."

Anderson drew up a chair, straddled it.

"This week, eh? So you figure we're putting the bee on you for the job you pulled last night."

If Balmer was nervous, he covered it pretty well.

"You got the wrong guy," he said. "Get me a drink of water, huh? Okay, I'll trot down to your crumby old jail."

WALT ANDERSON went to the bathroom, drew a glass of water, and returned smiling to the bedroom.

"Thanks," said Balmer, sitting up.

"You're so welcome," Anderson told him. He threw the contents into the crook's face. "Now snap into it, you cheap hood! I haven't got all day."

"Why, you—"

Anderson cuffed him across the mouth. He shut up. He dressed sullenly, bathed his slit lip in cold water—and slammed the apartment door in the policeman's face as they left.

Anderson cursed, swung the door open, but by this time Vince Balmer was headed up a corridor fire-escape toward the roof. When the lawman got to the top, Balmer was across the roof, all set to jump the narrow distance that separated the building from the next.

"Hold up!" Anderson yelled, lining up his gun sights.

Balmer jumped. The policeman's gun went off, and the slug caught the fleeing thug in the right thigh. The thug screamed, jerked his body half upright, and started to crawl toward a ventilator.

Anderson's next bullet clipped him in the wrist. Vince Balmer screamed again, but this time he didn't move. In a daze, he cursed himself for trying to escape without his gun. He didn't move much when Walt Anderson slapped tourniquets around his bleeding flesh and, in fact, he didn't move at all until an hour or so after the hospital blood transfusion.

He was still weak, but he shook his head determinedly as Johnny Harris pointed a lean finger at him. Herbert Miller, the over-padded mural painter, stood behind Harris, somewhat nonplussed.

And Policeman Walt Anderson had something in his hand. He glanced at it, and then he fastened his gaze on Balmer's lean, high-cheekboned face.

"Yep, it checks, just like when I first saw it," Anderson said with finality. "You got your portrait done in oils last night, Vince. For free," he told the white-faced thief. "Here—take a look."

Vince Balmer stared, his eyes wide and slightly glassy. This was his face, all right, painted with every feature distinct. The snub, upturned nose. The heavy eyelashes. The slight dimple in the chin. The high, sharp cheekbones. The little oil portrait in Anderson's hand was a masterpiece of its kind.

Balmer glared at Johnny Harris. "You did it, eh?"

Harris suppressed a tired yawn. "I'm afraid so. They say it checks with your picture in the police morgue. I sat up all night to get you down on canvas. After all, you didn't exactly pose for me, Balmer."

Muralist Herbert Miller clapped a fat hand to his forehead.

"The photographic touch!" he groaned. "Art for art's sake, heaven forbid! I must bow graciously to the inevitable."

After that, the long-haired boys couldn't do too much for Johnny Harris. They acclaimed him a true "artist," and threw a party in his honor. It was held in his apartment, and lasted the whole week-end.

They even let Harris pay for it out of the hundred dollars the bonding company gave him.

•

Dutcher was holding the gun, an automatic, steady in his hand

KILLER CURE

By VICTOR K. RAY

Trapped Detective Hogan needs a miracle to save him!

IT WAS hard staying far enough behind her so she wouldn't spot me. I kept wanting to break into a run. I wanted to catch up with her, take her by the arm, say, "Hello, baby. What are you doing on this side of town?"

Only I couldn't do that. She wouldn't be able to tell me that and I wouldn't be able to tell her what I was doing.

Watching Mary Sanders, I felt an ache in my throat. Her bright hair in the morning sun, the easy, graceful way she walked, the swing of her blue summer dress. That's what I could see. But I also had a picture of her straight little nose, her red lips, her quick green eyes.

She went into a meat market. I stopped, stared into a window. I didn't see what was in it. All I saw was my own reflection. My brown suit was wrinkled; my eyes had so much trouble in them I almost didn't recognize them. I told myself, a detective on the Force shouldn't have such worries.

In a few minutes, Mary came out. She stopped, looked back down Forest Avenue in my direction. She couldn't see me, because the awning was down low making a deep shade. I moved into the entrance of the store, watched her through the plate glass window. She looked for a long time, searchingly, carefully. Then she turned, walked on down Forest.

I followed more cautiously. She was

on the lookout for somebody tailing her. And that made everything worse.

At the end of the next block, she crossed Forest, went down the other side, to 1422 Forest Avenue. I watched her disappear in the doorway of the apartment house and I stood looking until my eyes hurt.

In my mind, I followed her, rode with her in the elevator to the third floor, walked with her down the hall to the front apartment. I could see her green eyes expectant, her mouth smiling perhaps, as the door opened cautiously. I could hear her deep voice saying something to the man who opened the door. A man named Dutcher Kohl.

Mary had rented the apartment four days ago, under the name of Mary Smith. She wasn't living in it. She was living at home, across town. But somebody was in there. Somebody for whom she bought groceries.

Good detective work on the part of one Burt Hogan? No, but a guy knows who his competition is. I knew mine was Dutcher Kohl. I'd known that a long time.

EVERY beat cop, every detective in town had Dutcher Kohl's description. They weren't straining their eyes for him because guys in the know said Dutcher Kohl had blown town. He wouldn't hang around with a murder rap waiting for him down at Headquarters, they said. Not Dutcher Kohl. So they were looking for him in Chicago, Detroit, Miami, and points east, west, north, and south.

Height: six feet one, the description read. Weight: about one-eighty. Color of hair: black. Eyes: light blue. Complexion: light. Straight nose, slightly cleft chin. Generally considered handsome, dresses well. Desperate, probably armed. Wanted for murder!

From the front entrance to the apartment house down the street I raised my eyes up to the awninged third-floor window. They were up there now. Dutcher Kohl, and a girl named Mary Sanders. Mary who, when she was nine, had said she would never speak to me again because I'd accidentally killed a June bug we were playing with.

I turned, walked back down Forest Avenue fast. I was running away. But I had to have time to work things out.

I was working on the case—on my own time. The case was cold. So was the kid, Anthony Franzetti. I kept remembering the white hospital room where he'd lain for three days. I kept hearing the sound of his breathing, until it had stopped.

He'd been picked up in a ditch beside his hijacked liquor truck, with the side of his skull crushed in. He'd lain in the hospital for seventy-two hours before he'd come to. He'd said, "It was Dutcher Kohl." I'd been there to hear it, and a corps of hospital doctors had been there to swear that the kid was sensible. It was enough to hang Dutcher Kohl. The kid had died six hours later.

I wished Mary could have been with me in the white hospital room watching the sheet rise and fall with Anthony Franzetti's last breath. Maybe she'd have a different angle on Dutcher Kohl now.

But maybe she'd keep saying what she'd always said, that Dutcher hadn't stood a chance, that his south side environment had cheated him out of a normal respect for law and order. All the excuses people give for guys like Dutcher Kohl.

Mary had been making those excuses since she'd first met him, when he was a young pool-room punk. Handsome, imaginative, he'd worked his way all the way up—to murder.

I got in my car two blocks down Forest Avenue, and drove home. This was my day off. I didn't have to make a report on my work.

But finally, they'd get Dutcher Kohl. The chances were Dutcher would take somebody with him. It might be Pete Madden, or George Hatcher, or Luther Norton. Or somebody else on the Force. I would say, "That was tough luck they had trying to bring Dutcher Kohl in." I would say, "It's hard to take a guy holed up in an apartment."

I wondered if I would say, "I knew he was there all the time. Sure, a girl I know was helping him hide out." Not likely.

I sat on the edge of my bed, and thought about it.

I could go down to Headquarters now, tell them all about it. I could say, "I've been watching a girl who goes by the name of Mary Smith. She's got an apartment over on Forest Avenue. I think she's hiding Dutcher Kohl." Then we'd go to the place with tear gas and riot guns—the way we do those things. My bet was that Dutcher Kohl would still take one or two with him, because he was that good with a gun.

But we'd have one Mary Smith on our hands, for being an accessory, for aiding and abetting a criminal guilty of murder. We'd find out right away that her real name was Mary Sanders.

I picked up the telephone, and called Mary's house. For a minute, I had a blind, unreasonable idea that she'd be there. But her mother answered.

She said, "Mary left early this morning, Burt. She went downtown shopping. She said she might take in a movie."

I said, "Ask her to call me when she comes in, Mrs. Sanders."

"All right," Mrs. Sanders said pleasantly. "How is everything, Burt? You haven't been around for quite awhile."

"Everything's fine, Mrs. Sanders."

I HUNG up, and moved around my apartment, forgetting about lunch, trying to think out my problems. But they weren't the kind I could think my way out of.

I was waiting for that phone call. The telephone in the next apartment rang. I had my hand on my telephone before I could calm down. Noises from the street filtered in. A car backfired, and I jumped.

I thought about Mary being an accessory. She even had an alias. Then I thought about me, Burt Hogan. How much can a cop know that he doesn't tell before he too becomes an accessory? That was a harder problem.

If I could only see Mary, I thought, and talk to her.

The doorbell rang. I stood for a minute with the telephone in my hand. I put it down, went into my living room, across to the door. I opened it.

Mary stood in the hall. Her green eyes had a distant, numbed look. A strand of her yellow hair had fallen down along her cheek.

"Mary!" I opened the door wide, took her arm, led her in.

"I was just passing," she said softly. "I thought I'd stop. I haven't seen you for awhile, Burt."

"I just called you," I said. "I left word with your mother for you to call back."

"Oh?" She sat down in the big leather chair uncertainly. "I haven't been home."

I pulled the leather hassock up alongside the chair. "What's wrong, Mary? You look worried."

"Wrong? Nothing. I'm just tired. I walked back from downtown. I've been to a movie. It was a Humphrey Bogart movie, where he got mixed up with a girl, and there was a murder, and—"

"Stop it, Mary. You don't have to prove to me that you went to a movie. Save that for your mother."

She looked at me quickly. "No, you never ask me for proof about anything, do you, Burt? If I say it, that's enough. . . ." Her voice trailed off.

I got up, moved over to the window, waiting for her to go on. I thought it might be easier for her to tell me what she had come for if I wasn't so close to her, wasn't looking directly into her eyes.

"Have they found him, Burt?" she asked abruptly. "Have they got a lead on where he is?"

"They're looking for him in Detroit and Chicago," I said. "They haven't got a lead. Guys in the know say he's left town." I looked at her. She held her hands in her lap, rubbing them together. She didn't look up at me.

"They'll kill him when they find him, won't they?" she said. "They won't try to take him alive."

"They'll try to take him alive," I said. "They almost always try." I kept my tone flat and detached, talking about "they" like I wasn't one of them. "But they'll probably kill him, because he'll make them."

I went back to her, knelt down beside the big chair. "He's a murderer, Mary!" My voice was harsh, strained. I took her by the shoulder, made her look at me. "He killed a kid named Anthony

Franzetti just for the fun of it. He didn't have to. He could have used a sap instead of an iron bar. That would have been enough. But he killed him, Mary. I watched the kid die. How can you keep on carrying the torch for a murderer?"

Her mouth trembled. "Dutcher never had a chance, Burt."

I got up. "Mary! You can't go on saying that. He killed a man. You've got to stop making excuses somewhere."

She got up out of the chair, went across to the door. "I'll go, Burt. I guess I'm pretty tired."

SHE put her hand on the knob uncertainly, stood there for a minute not seeming to know whether she wanted to go or stay.

I watched her. She'd come by to see how near the police were to finding him, to see if maybe we'd tumbled to the fact that she was hiding him. And she'd expected me to tell her if we had.

"I'm sorry I bothered you with my troubles," she said softly, opening the door.

"Wait a minute, Mary. I'll drive you home."

We went down, got in my car. She sat far over in her corner of the seat. Her face was white and drawn, her eyes were dead. I drove slow to her house. Mary was like a stranger.

Her mother was in the front yard watering flowers. She came out to the car when we stopped in front. She was a tall, graying woman, a little heavy. Full of good humor.

"I'm glad you found her, Burt," she said. "I hope you can snap my little girl out of it. She's been moping around for days. She quit her job last week. I don't know what's wrong."

I looked at Mary. She managed a little smile for her mother.

I said, "Maybe I can do something about that." But I knew I couldn't. "How are the flowers?" I asked.

"They're fine," Mrs. Sanders replied. "But I've missed your help around here on Sunday mornings. All that digging, at my age!" She laughed. Mrs. Sanders was all right.

"You should put your daughter at digging," I said. "That would snap her out of it."

Mrs. Sanders went on talking about her flowers. Mary didn't have anything to say. She got out, and left Mrs. Sanders talking to me.

Then in a minute, Mary's little brother, Jimmy, came galloping around the corner of the house. He was wearing his cowboy suit.

"Whoa!" he yelled. He slid his imaginary horse to a halt, and with his hand down on his toy gun. "Hi, Burt!"

"Hello, Jimmy. Having much Indian trouble these days?"

"It's not the Indians that are bothering me," he said. "It's the rustlers."

Jimmy was still carrying the ammunition I'd made for him. Regular .38 caliber ammunition; nothing less was good enough for Jimmy. I'd removed the powder, and filled the cartridges with salt.

I stayed long enough to be polite.

Mrs. Sanders said, "Come back to see us more often, Burt. Come any time."

"I guess I ought to wait until Mary invites me," I said.

"Nonsense," said Mrs. Sanders. "I'm inviting you. Jimmy and I want you to come."

"I'll come."

"Burt, I'm worried about Mary. She's so changed lately." Mrs. Sanders' eyes were troubled.

"She'll snap out of it," I said. "Everybody has their troubles now and then."

"I hope she'll be all right, Burt."

I drove away. I looked back, and she turned around slowly, and just stood there. She seemed to have forgotten her flowers.

Well, now I'd seen Mary. I'd talked to her. She had lied, and I had lied, by the things we hadn't said. We were farther apart than ever.

I went home. I sat down in the big leather chair where Mary had sat. I kept thinking about Dutcher Kohl, in that apartment across town. How far can a cop go without becoming an accessory, himself? I knew I'd already gone too far. I couldn't put it off any longer.

I walked downstairs to the street. I got in my car, drove down South Grand in the direction of Forest Avenue. Darkness was beginning to move out of the alleys into the street; the street lights came on. My tires whispered along the concrete. The already cooling air touched my face. I was sweating.

I parked on Forest, near 1422 Forest Avenue.

I looked up at the windows of the third floor front apartment. The lights were on behind drawn shades. Maybe Mary's up there now, I thought. Maybe she'd rushed right back over to tell him the good news. Dutcher, they're looking for you in Detroit and Chicago, and points east, west, north, and south.

I had a sick feeling in my stomach. I had a sudden impulse to start my car again and drive and keep driving.

I MADE myself get out. I went into the vestibule. A heavy, red-haired woman carrying a paper sack filled with bottled beer pushed the buzzer to her apartment. I caught the door as it clicked unlocked, held it open for her. She said, "Thanks, honey."

Smell of old varnish on old wood; percussion of my footsteps on worn stairs; dirty, handprinted walls.

I stopped on the landing at the third floor. A door led into the hall. Through the dirty glass, I could see across the hall to the door of the front apartment. I stopped for a minute.

I heard a movement behind me on the stairs leading up to the fourth floor. I felt a gun hard against my back.

I looked around slowly into Dutcher Kohl's face. There was a hard, flat quality in his eyes, a lack of animation in the pupils. It's something that comes with being a killer, maybe.

"Just so there wouldn't be any surprises for anybody except you, Hogan," he breathed, "I appointed myself a committee of one to greet you. I saw you drive up."

"I wasn't trying not to be seen, Dutcher."

"Straight ahead. Right through the door, and across the hall."

I walked ahead of him. I put my hand down on the knob of his door, turned it, walked in. I looked around the room.

Mary wasn't here. I let my breath out slowly.

Dutcher Kohl closed the door behind him, and clicked the lock. He kept his eyes on me.

The gun, an automatic, was steady in his hand.

"I've got a proposition, Dutcher." My throat ached as I said the words. I turned, faced him. "Put up the gun," I said.

"A proposition from a cop," said Dutcher. He laughed a low, mirthless laugh. "I'll hold the gun. Sit on the divan, there." He motioned with the gun.

I sat down.

Dutcher's mouth pulled in a tight grin.

"What's the proposition, Hogan?"

"Get out of town." My voice was raspy, shaky. "Leave now. I'll forget about your being here."

"And what do I give you in return for this generous offer?" he asked.

"You don't give me anything."

"You're noble, you are." He laughed again. "You want me to give you Mary Sanders. That's great." He clapped his free hand down on the side of his leg. "Wait till I tell her!"

"I want you to give her back to her family, back to a life of her own."

"You're good, Hogan," he said. "Always handing out those high sounding sentiments."

I sat there. My throat ached with distaste for this thing I was doing. And now, it seemed, it wasn't going to work, after all.

"Then you won't leave?" I asked.

"I'd be a fool to leave, Hogan. This is the coolest town in the country for me. You followed Mary Sanders here, but you're the only cop in town who would. And you won't do anything about it."

I sat there, feeling the sweat run down, soak into my collar, wondering if I could do anything about it.

"Because," he went on, spacing his words slowly, deliberately, so I would get the full meaning, "you wouldn't want Mary to get sent up for helping me." He scratched his chin with the barrel of his gun. "No, Hogan. Thanks very much. But I think I'll stick around."

"That was your chance, Dutcher," I said. "You had it."

GRIMLY I got up to go. I'd tried to compromise, but it hadn't worked. I guess it never does. Well, at least, I knew it now. I wouldn't try it again. I was through wondering what I was going to do. I knew. Someway, somehow, I was going to take Dutcher Kohl in.

I looked at him. He held his gun leveled at my head; his knuckles were white around it. I realized suddenly I'd made a mistake. Because behind the gun muzzle, in his eyes, I saw what he meant to do. No time for talk now. No time for compromise. I'd made a mistake.

He'd said he was going to stay and take his chances. Only he didn't mean to. A killer can't take any chances; the stakes are too high. But more than that. Regardless of the stakes, he would still kill me because he was a killer. It was in his blood. I could see it in his eyes. He was going to do it, here, now, the way he'd done with Anthony Franzetti.

Then I heard the flat, futile snap a gun makes when it misfires, when it fails to go off.

There was an instant of surprise when both of us were unable to move. I looked at the gun gripped in Dutcher's hand. It had given me a reprieve from death. A miracle.

Before I could move, I heard it snap again.

In Dutcher's eyes was disappointment, and something else.

Then I threw myself forward. I felt the gun come down, sending sharp pain down the side of my head. I hit him, felt his flesh give against my knuckles. The room was spinning for me as we stood in the middle of it, slugging it out, a grinding, painful, nightmarish experience. Then Dutcher Kohl went down and my gun was against his head. The room stopped whirling.

He kept saying over and over, "Don't, don't, please don't!"

I called Headquarters. It was all a reflex, a routine. I was still thinking of what had happened. It was running around in my head like a squirrel in a cage.

I went across the room, picked up Dutcher Kohl's gun. I held it in my hand, remembering what it had done. A deadly weapon, they say. It had saved my life.

Holding that gun, I got a funny feeling. I guess there isn't a cop in the world who hasn't felt at some time or another that a miracle saved his life. He stays home one night because he's got a bad cold, and the guy who walks his beat for him gets shot. You never know where the miracle began.

But here was something tangible, a gun that hadn't worked. A gun in the hands of a gun expert like Dutcher Kohl —and still it hadn't worked.

I held it in my hand, feeling the sweat break out, make the metal slick.

I flicked the cylinder out; the cartridges fell into my hand. Regular .38 caliber ammunition. But they hadn't gone off. Then I looked at them closer and felt a ripple go up my back. The cartridges were bright and shiny—from being carried in a kid's cartridge belt.

And I realized it was more than a miracle because they were regular .38 caliber ammunition, and they were filled with salt. Mary Sanders had put her little brother's dud cartridges in Dutcher's gun.

She'd saved my life! It was that simple. It canceled out everything. Maybe. I thought about it some more.

A PICTURE of Mary kept getting in front of me, with her white face, her dead eyes, and a strand of her blonde hair on her cheek. The way she had looked when she'd come to my apartment today. I could hear her ragged voice saying, "They'll kill him when they find him, won't they?" And after that, I could hear my own voice saying, "They'll probably kill him, because he'll make them."

But there was more. She'd rented an apartment for him. She'd done his shopping for him. She hadn't turned him over to the police.

Sure, she'd saved my life. But it was no good. The evidence was all on the other side.

She'd saved Dutcher Kohl's life.

She'd put her little brother's dud bullets in his gun to keep him from forcing the police to kill him. Saving my life had been only incidental.

Maybe.

I didn't know.

I could say in my report, "Dutcher Kohl was aided and abetted in hiding out by Mary Sanders." Or I could say, he was "aided and abetted in hiding out by one Mary Smith, who rented the apartment, but who has so far eluded capture."

I couldn't make my report right away. I had to see her.

Pete Madden and George Hatcher arrived. I let them have Dutcher Kohl and got out fast. I ran down the stairs, pushed out the door. The cool night air hit my face. I stopped.

My car was parked a couple of doors down to the right. On the car door, I could see a girl's sleeve. Mary's. She was waiting. I walked down toward the car, feeling a kind of numbness in my legs. I went around to the street side, slid under the wheel.

Mary turned to face to me, reached out with one hand to my arm. "It's you, Burt. I'm so glad." Her voice was husky, a little ragged.

It came to me then that she hadn't known who would come out until just now. Because even if Dutcher Kohl's gun was loaded with dud cartridges, he might get away, and it would be my car he would use for his getaway.

Then I saw the little gun in her lap. She'd been waiting. For either one of us. And she'd come prepared.

She looked at me. Her gaze broke suddenly as she realized I was looking at the gun in her lap. She put it in her purse.

She started to explain. "I was waiting. I thought maybe he—"

"You don't have to tell me," I said.

"I've got to, Burt." Her voice was firm. "I've got to explain this, because I almost made a terrible mistake. When you were following me this morning—"

"You knew I was following you?"

"Yes. I wouldn't have noticed you, except that it was a strange part of town to me, and I guess unconsciously I was looking for someone familiar. And I saw you. You were a block away, but I recognized you. Then I realized why you were there. And that made everything different. Before, it was just Dutcher, and he was running, and he needed me. Even though it was murder, it still seemed far away to me. I didn't know Anthony Franzetti."

I had the feeling she was explaining it to herself, as much as to me.

"But when you were in it," she went on, "it came close. Now, I was part of it, and I was on the wrong side, the side opposite you, Burt. I guess it made me know how much I wanted to be on your side."

Her green eyes held mine. Behind them, there was happiness.

"But I wouldn't ever have done what I did, if I'd thought he was really guilty of murder," she said. "Somehow I couldn't believe it." Her hand groped for mine in the seat beside her. I took hold of it. She went on:

"But tonight, when I put the dud bullets in Dutcher's gun, it suddenly came to me that I'd made the big decision. I knew he was a killer, and that he would kill again, if it were necessary. Because if I didn't think he was a killer, why would I feel it was necessary to put dud bullets in his gun?"

I sat there for a minute, the clean feeling moving through me. Sure, just like I'd let love get in my eyes, and blot out things that should have been fundamental, Mary had let the faith she'd had in a guy we'd both known when we were kids get in the way, too.

She came over from the curb side. Some of the color was back in her cheeks. Some of the life was back in her green eyes.

I waited until the next morning to make my report.

•

FROM THE ARCHIVES OF

SCOTLAND YARD

The mere mention of the words "Scotland Yard" conjures up a picture of a busy and efficient center of crime solution, highlighted by memories of great detectives and famous cases. It brings back to mind Sherlock Holmes and Baker Street, countless heroes of fact and fiction, enveloped in an aura of mystery and glamour. In this new series of stories about the Yard, we will bring you the true facts—an actual "inside" glimpse into the workings of the organization, based on real cases—not legend!

CLUE of the

FEW crime organizations have achieved the world-wide reputation of the men of Scotland Yard. Its name dates back to the tenth century when a fortress in London used by visiting Scottish kings became known as Scotland Yard. Centuries later, when the fortress was turned over for police use, the name stuck. When the present group of police buildings was constructed in 1890 on the Thames embankment, it was called officially New

The strange story of Mrs. Fox and her devoted son, and how Scotland Yard refused to call an accident an accident—without full proof!

HORSEHAIR by JACKSON HITE

Scotland Yard, but to the world it still is known as Scotland Yard, home of the famous C.I.D., Criminal Investigation Department.

One of the reasons for the Yard's preeminence as a crime fighting organization has been its leadership in scientific police studies. Scotland Yard, for example, was the first law enforcement agency to use fingerprints as a means of identifying perpetrators of a crime. Today many noted scientists are affiliated with it and others have made themselves available at the Yard's beck and call.

High Ability Wins Promotion

Its noted CID Inspectors have been chosen purely on a basis of ability and not political pull. They are men trained to think all around a problem so they can attack it from many angles, and in case after case they have shown a remarkable willingness to perform strange experiments in order to arrive at the truth. One of these included the charring of a piece of carpeting and burning some horsehair, one of the Yard's "blue-ribbon" cases.

On the brisk afternoon of October 16, 1929, a couple arrived at the leading hotel in Margate, an English seacoast resort town. The season was over and only a few people were registered in the hotel. The pair were a striking couple. The woman was frail and gray-haired and walked with a shuffling gait. She obviously was in poor health but nonetheless held herself very erect and moved with a graceful air.

Accompanying her was a younger man, about thirty years old. There was a marked resemblance between the two and it was apparent that he was the woman's son. He was almost too handsome for a man, having regular features set off by piercing blue eyes and wavy dark blond hair.

The Foxes Take Suite

They had arrived by taxi but had no luggage with them. The man registered as Sidney Harris Fox, and his mother, Mrs. Rosaline Fox. He explained that they were traveling to Lyndhurst but that he decided to stop over for a few days to see if the sea air might do his mother some good. Because he had made this decision rather suddenly while en route, their luggage already had gone on ahead.

The experienced hotel manager noted the impeccable Bond Street cut of Fox's clothes, his ease of bearing and obvious refinement and gave a sign to the clerk to allow them to register.

Fox was most solicitous of his mother's comfort and, since he had his choice of many suites, took his time selecting one that would get the morning sun, was sheltered from any sea breezes, and contained a gas heater in the fireplace which his mother could light to remove any chill from the room. The suite he chose had one door leading to the public corridor with an inner door connecting the two adjoining bedrooms.

Margate is Friendly Town

Margate at that time of year was typical of most resort towns in off-season. The permanent population was small and only a few of the necessity shops kept open all year long. During these off months the hotel served as social center for the town residents. The atmosphere was more like a club, with almost everybody in town knowing everybody else, the few guests in the hotel sharing in the congenial atmosphere.

Fox fitted into the social life most readily. A fluent and entertaining speaker, he had a fund of stories to tell and, although his conversation contained ready references to titled friends and others whose names were known far beyond London, he neither put on airs nor acted in any condescending manner to his listeners. He was highly regarded by all those he met and was a most welcome addition to the hotel guests.

His adoration of his mother soon was the talk of the town. He seldom left her side, walking with her, dining with her, and spending the evenings playing cards or reading to her. Only after she had fallen asleep would he come downstairs to the lobby where he would entertain the others. His mother was an alert woman and a charming conversationalist despite her illness.

Mrs. Fox Collapses

Although he had intended to stop at the hotel just for two days, he decided to stay on a little longer because the traveling had so tired his mother. On Sunday, October 20, Fox had a scare when he rang up the manager and asked him to summon the nearest doctor because his mother seemed to have fainted. The physician assured him that he had needlessly alarmed himself and that his mother was in fairly good shape considering her lengthy illness.

Reassured, Fox left the following day for a business trip to London, but first summoned several hotel employees and wrung from them a promise that they would look in frequently and take care of his mother until he returned. Before he left he asked the desk clerk to cash a two-pound check for his railroad fare, but was refused because it was against the rules of the hotel. Fox went down the street to a pharmacist whose acquaintance he had made during his brief visit and the druggist cashed the check for him.

He arrived in London that evening and while still at the railroad station telephoned the hotel to inquire after his mother. He was informed that she had passed a restful day. The following morning Fox again rang to make certain that everything was going smoothly.

Mother Seems Stronger

He returned to Margate on the 23rd and, after visiting his mother and finding her in good spirits, came down to the desk and informed the manager that he thought she would be strong enough for them to continue their journey the following morning.

The pair had spent just one week in Margate and during that time Fox had won a host of admiring friends for his thoughtful treatment of his 63-year-old widowed mother.

"There's few lads like him these days," many Margate residents commented with beaming approval.

That evening Fox instructed the manager to have his bill ready in the morning. He revealed he was so pleased with his mother's condition that he had promised her some wine after dinner. None of the brands carried in the hotel taproom were to his liking and so he went out and purchased half a bottle of port at a nearby wine shop. He also bought her an evening paper.

Invalid Reads Paper

A short time later Fox returned to the lobby and guests who inquired about his mother learned that he was allowing her to stay up that night. She had promised to go to bed as soon as she finished the paper. The rest of the evening passed quietly enough at the hotel. The few guests sat about talking, joined as usual by some of the town merchants and residents. By 10:30 most of them had departed and shortly before 11 o'clock Fox went up to his room to retire for the night.

About a half hour later the guests in the hotel were electrified by a man shouting, "Fire!"

Racing down the steps was Fox dressed in his pajamas. Semi-hysterical, he shouted for help, begging assistance for his mother trapped in her blazing room.

Several of the guests, including a traveling salesman, rushed to Fox's suite. Thick, pungent smoke was beginning to seep from under the cracks of the door. The men entered the first room and found that the door to Mrs. Fox's bedroom was closed. When the traveling salesman flung her door open the room was so smoke-filled that he couldn't see into it. Tying a handkerchief over his mouth, the heroic salesman groped his way about until he found Mrs. Fox unconscious on the bed. He picked up the frail woman and carried her out to the hall.

Try to Revive Mrs. Fox

While waiting for a physician to arrive, several of the guests tried to revive the woman without success. The night clerk, assisted by several other employees, succeeded in extinguishing the flames before the arrival of the fire fighters. The fire seemed to have been centered beneath a smouldering stuffed chair drawn up near the gas heater. The newspaper and several pieces of Mrs. Fox's clothing were burned.

A physician worked over the stricken woman for over an hour before he finally admitted defeat. Mrs. Fox was dead.

Fox was dazed at the news. He sat there staring at the doctor as if not understanding and then, when realization of what the words meant swept over him, he broke into convulsive sobs and required medical attention.

He explained to police that he had gone to sleep when he came upstairs. The light was out in his mother's room and he didn't open her door because he was afraid he might disturb her. She was a very light sleeper.

He was awakened by smoke coming into his room. He opened the door to the adjoining bedroom and when he choked upon the acrid smoke hurriedly closed it and dashed down to the lobby for help, not even pausing to don a robe.

"Accidental," The Jury Says

At the inquest held the following day it was suggested that Mrs. Fox had been reading in the chair in front of the gas heater. When she stood up to go to bed, the paper had fallen near the heater and become ignited and, in turn, had started the smouldering blaze under the chair. Unaware of what was happening she had gone to sleep and was overcome by the smoke.

A jury returned with a verdict of accidental death and Fox left with the body of his mother for Great Frensham in Norfolk where she was buried in the village churchyard. Before the grief stricken son left he asked the manager to forward all bills to him.

Several days later Scotland Yard entered the case. Chief Inspector Hambrook and Detective Sergeant Ayto traveled to Margate and began to make inquiries.

The Scotland Yard officers had no knowledge that Mrs. Fox had not died an accidental death, but they were curious about two strange episodes. The first was that the two-pound check Fox had cashed with the pharmacist had bounced. Fox had no account at the bank. The second was that Mrs. Fox carried a 1,000-pound insurance policy on her life. This policy had been due to expire several days before her death, and Fox had renewed it on his visit to London, a visit made possible by the forged check. He had not as yet paid his hotel bill.

Residents Defend Fox

Everywhere the men of Scotland Yard went they met with the same story of complete devotion by the son to his mother. It was unthinkable for any of them to consider that Fox had burned his mother alive for the insurance money. They were certain that her death just after he renewed the policy was an unfortunate coincidence.

The Scotland Yard officers kept their own counsel. Without being aware that any probe was being conducted into his mother's death, Fox was arrested on the bad check charge and held for trial.

Meanwhile, Scotland Yard was checking into the background of the prisoner. This was his third arrest for issuing bad checks. The officers learned that Fox had been born in Great Frensham but when he was in his early 'teens had been taken in tow by a wealthy titled Englishman who hired him as a servant and took him to London. Fox was a handsome boy with blond curly hair and he soon became a favorite with the callers at the house.

Shortly after World War I broke out Fox's employer died. Fox now was 18 years old and obtained a position with a bank but left hurriedly and joined the Army when he was discovered to be short in his accounts. In the Army he became friendly with an officer who took him on visits where he met a number of titled and other important people. In an effort to impress some of those he met, he hinted that he was the illegitimate son of a nobleman and began to write a series of forged checks to underwrite lavish parties he gave. He was caught and given a short jail sentence. Even then his concern was to keep the news from his mother who now was working in London in order to be near her favorite son.

His Checks Were Phony

After his discharge from the Army he worked for a bank, forged another check and wound up doing his second prison bit. He tried the same thing after his release and went to jail again, a longer term this time.

The Scotland Yard officers were particularly interested in one item they turned up. Shortly after his release from his third term in prison Fox met a wealthy Australian woman who had come to England in order that her children might attend school there. Although she was a much older woman than Fox, the young man made love to her and at his suggestion she took out an insurance policy on her life, naming him as beneficiary.

The woman also made out a will in which she stated that she owed Fox some money but that the insurance covered the payment. She did this at Fox's request who pointed out that if anything did happen to her someone might question his right to be named beneficiary in the policy. The note in the will, he suggested, would prevent any awkward situation from arising.

Open Gas Jet

Not too long after she took out the policy the woman drank some wine Fox had brought her and fell asleep much earlier than usual. She awoke quite ill and discovered that the illuminating gas jet was on and the poisonous gas was flooding the room. The woman considered the entire episode an accident. She canceled the policy some time later when Fox was named co-respondent in a divorce suit.

By now the Scotland Yard officers were more interested than ever. They examined the room in which Mrs. Fox had died with great care. A small bottle of gasoline had been in the bedroom, but this was not out of the ordinary since many people in those days used gasoline as a spot remover to clean garments. The carpet and the felt pad beneath it were badly burned while the floor boards were charred.

The officers used the gasoline for a series of experiments. They found out what kind of garments Mrs. Fox had worn and obtained samples just like them. Some of these garments were ignited by the gas heater and placed on the carpet. They burned without much heat and slightly charred the rug. Those placed beneath the stuffed chair made no headway against the tightly packed horsehair with which the chair was stuffed.

Detectives Continue Experiments

Other garments were soaked with gasoline and then set on fire on the carpet. These burned right through and the hot blaze also set the horsehair in the chair smouldering, giving off a choking smoke.

Satisfied with the tests of the horsehair, Inspector Hambrook obtained a court order for the exhuming of the body of Mrs. Fox. Sir Bernard Spilsbury, noted pathologist for Scotland Yard, performed the autopsy.

His report told Hambrook and his assistant that they had been on the right path after all. The doctor found no soot in the woman's windpipe. This indicated that she might have been dead before the fire broke out and her room filled with the smoke. It was not conclusive proof, however, since she could have been stricken with a heart attack when she discovered the fire and died before she had inhaled too much of the smoke. Dr. Spilsbury, however, had another test to perform, one first perfected by Dr. Alexander O. Gettler, chief toxicologist for the New York City Medical Examiner's office.

The dead woman's blood was checked for carbon monoxide and no trace of any was found in the blood. Dr. Gettler's tests have shown that any victim who dies during a fire inhales some of the deadly carbon fume which finds its way into the bloodstream, but no carbon monoxide can enter the bloodstream after death. Methods have been perfected to detect even the slightest trace of it in the blood.

Find Bruises on Tongue

Dr. Spilsbury was able to state that Mrs. Fox was dead before the fire broke out in her room.

The autopsy also brought to light a small bruise on Mrs. Fox's tongue, the kind of bruise made when a person bites down hard on her tongue. Mrs. Fox wore false teeth and under ordinary conditions would not be able to inflict the kind of bruise she had, but Inspector Hambrook knew that when a person suffocates or is being strangled her tongue protrudes between the teeth and the jaws clench in death agony, producing such bruises on the tongue. The autopsy, however, showed no bruises on the neck to indicate manual strangulation. Dr. Spilsbury said that none are necessarily present when a person is smothered with a pillow.

The picture was becoming clear to the officers. Mrs. Fox had been asleep when the killer entered. She may have been drugged by something in the wine so she could not resist the attack. The killer placed a pillow over her nose and mouth and held it there until she suffocated. He then staged the fire scene, waited until the room filled with smoke and dashed out shouting for help. So far as they were concerned, the killer was Fox, the devoted son.

Scotland Yard Goes Slowly

Despite the conclusions of the officers, Scotland Yard did not leap into action. More tests were performed with horsehair, some being burned in tight bunches, others held in loose clumps. Finally, on January 9, 1930, more than two months after his mother had died Fox was charged with her murder. He thought he had been taken from his cell in connection with the bad check charge and was shocked when the accusation was leveled against him.

"How could you ever think such a thing?" he demanded. "I loved my mother more than anything else in the world. I never would have killed her."

All the evidence, of course, was circumstantial, and the history of criminal trials has proven that experts disagree and, to each expert brought forth by Scotland Yard defense attorneys, counter with experts of their own who dispute the findings of the opposing side.

Fox Dolls Up For Trial

The strange spectacle of a son being accused of murdering his mother, when his devotion to her was widely known, captured the public imagination and opinion was sharply divided as to his possible guilt. This interest was further heightened by the fact that English juries are slow to convict on purely circumstantial evidence. Fox, of course, denied that he had killed his mother and insisted that she had died either as a result of the fire or of her illness. It was up to the men of Scotland Yard to prove to a jury otherwise and this proof would have to be most conclusive in a case of suspected matricide.

Fox was dressed in his usual fashion-plate style when he was placed on trial at the Lewes Assizes. His dark gray gloves matched his overcoat and he wore a dark blue pin-stripe suit.

In his opening address to the jury the prosecutor revealed that when Fox had gone to London he had renewed the policy for only a few days and that the insurance would have expired at midnight, less than an hour before Mrs. Fox had died. In addition to the officers of Scotland Yard, he presented as witnesses the chief officers of the Margate Fire Brigade and Dr. Spilsbury.

The following question was put to the fire chief:

"Fully conscious as you are of the seriousness of this question, I want you to tell the jury what conclusion your experiments have led you to with regard to the origin of the fire in Mrs. Fox's room. Do you or do you not think the fire could have been accidental?"

"I can only say that I cannot find any means of its being an accidental fire," was his reply.

No Smoke in Lungs

Dr. Spilsbury's testimony was typically blunt.

"If a person had been alive when there was any appreciable quantity of smoke in that room, must you have found minute particles of smoke or soot in the windpipe?" he was asked.

His reply came in one word. "Yes."

"Are you able to say whether Mrs. Fox had died before there was any appreciable quantity of smoke in that room?"

"Yes, she did."

"Do you think such a woman as Mrs. Fox, possibly sleeping, would be able to put up much of a resistance?"

"No."

"Supposing you had a case of strangulation by a pillow placed with one hand upon the face, obstructing the mouth and nostrils, and the neck held in position, as it were, would you get the symptoms you have found here?"

"Yes, under these conditions it would be impossible for the victim to move her neck."

With the foundation for the smoke in the room laid by the questioning of the previous witnesses, the experts from Scotland Yard were placed on the witness stand and demonstrated in the courtroom to the jury the tests they had performed with horsehair, bunched exactly as it was in the stuffed chair in the bedroom.

Gasoline Fire Indicated

Their demonstration clearly indicated that only an intense heat could cause the hair to smoulder the way it had in Mrs. Fox's bedroom and the few garments that had burned at the time of her death did not give off sufficient heat unless they were saturated with gasoline. The newspaper had been too far from the chair to ignite the stuffing. Similar tests were performed for the jury with pieces of carpet.

Fox took the stand in his own behalf and the prosecution forced him to admit episodes in his past including a history of theft which began when he still was an elementary school student in Great Frensham. He stole a collection box from a charity organization and then went about pretending to be collecting funds for the charity, but actually pocketing the money. Because of his extreme youth at the time no criminal charges were filed against him, but he was whipped for his deed.

But Fox could not be made to admit that he had murdered his mother. When asked why he had fled down the stairs when he thought his mother was in danger of burning to death in the adjoining room, he explained that he had lost his head in the excitement.

Fox Explains Glibly

"Can you explain to me why you closed the door to your mother's room instead of flinging it wide open?" he was asked.

"My explanation is that I did it so that the smoke would not spread into the hotel," he replied.

Throughout his testimony he spoke of his love for his mother. She had been in an infirmary in Portsmouth for over a year following a stroke. Unable to bear the separation any longer, he had taken her out of the infirmary on March 27 and from then until her death they had been traveling about. A parade of witnesses also testified of the close companionship between mother and son. But Fox remained silent when asked to explain away the tests performed by the Scotland Yard officers in the courtroom in front of the jury.

He was found guilty of first degree murder.

When asked if he had anything to say before sentence was pronounced, Fox replied, "I never murdered my mother."

He was led to the gallows on April 8, 1930. "I ask for no personal sympathy," he declared just before the trap was sprung. He received none from the witnesses who were certain that he was guilty of a most macabre crime brought to light by the shrewd work of Scotland Yard.

ANOTHER TRUE STORY FROM THE ARCHIVES OF SCOTLAND YARD

THE GREAT PEARL THEFT

COMING IN THE NEXT ISSUE!

MY VOTE'S FOR

Dwight and Gail Berke start adding up the clues in a mystery case and get a total that checks with crime!

CHAPTER I

Body in the Shower

IT WAS exactly nine o'clock on Wednesday night when Dwight Berke, sports editor of the *Journal*, moved his lean frame into the Hotel Broadview elevator. His wife, Gail, her four-by-five Graflex slung over her tailored shoulder by its shiny strap, followed him.

Berke grinned at the elevator boy and shoved his snap-brim back off his crisp red hair in a way he had. "I'm Di Berke of the *Journal*. I'm looking for a blonde honey by the name of Honey Hendrix. The world's best woman bowler. Eight-eighteen, I think the clerk said."

MURDER

They found Rose McGuire lying on a leather divan—dead!

a novelet by

CARL G. HODGES

The operator pursed his lips and uttered a low wolf whistle. "She wastes a classy chassis knockin' over ten pins. She knocks the men for a loop, too. But she ain't in Eight-eighteen."

"I want a story and my wife wants pix for a sport feature. Where is she?"

"She's on ten. The radio studio. WDAY. Mike Reynard's throwing a party for the Mayor and some of the political bigwigs. Kind of a victory celebration for Mayor Nance and the commissioners. Honey Hendrix is there; she's here from Detroit visiting Mike Reynard. He's her brother, you know."

Gail tugged at Di's sleeve. "I'll feel like a fool breaking into a stag party. A political stag, at that."

Di grinned. "Honey Hendrix is no stag, baby. You heard what the boy said."

Gail sniffed and tossed her pert head so her curls bounced. "She's a lady bowler. She's probably all muscles and smokes cigars."

The operator chuckled wisely. "Yeah, but what muscles." The elevator stopped on ten and he slid the door open. "This is it, folks. Straight ahead till you see the sign."

As they turned down the hall, a man's tweeded figure brushed rudely past them, knocking Gail and her camera against the wall. Di reached out a brown hand and jerked the man backward. The stench of hard liquor blasted into his face as red eyes peered at him and a blurred voice said:

"Shorry. So shorry. Apologize lady."

Di said, "Okay, Duffy. On your way. And you better quit hitting the bottle with Blair Summers and Luke Street or you'll be even too rotten for that yellow rag you work for."

Duffy opened his mouth to retort. Then his eyes bleared and showed fear and he ducked his head as if he thought Di was going to smack him. He tipped his hat with fumbling fingers and lumbered clumsily into the elevator.

GAIL readjusted her camera on its strap. "Such friends you've got. Who's the walking distillery?"

"One of our colleagues of the fourth estate. Ted Duffy. He's political editor of the *Banner*. He's been on a jag since yesterday. He and Summers and Street. Summers has a suite here on ten some place. It was his mayoralty campaign headquarters. He thought three years with the OPA would help him to win. Duffy backed him in the *Banner*. They've been soaked to the gills since the returns started to come in last night. Dave Nance beat him hands down."

Gail said, "I can figure Summers. He lost the race for mayor. I can figure Duffy. He backed the wrong candidate. But where does Luke Street come in? I thought he was one of Nance's fair-haired boys."

"He was during Nance's first term, but Nance got word he was playing tag with both sides of the ballot, making sure of his job as superintendent of streets. The first thing Nance did when the returns started coming in last night was to announce he was firing Street."

Gail shivered. "Politics! What a breeding-ground for hate!"

"You're not kidding, baby. In politics they love you one day and shoot you the next."

By this time they had reached a neon sign, unlighted now because the station was off the air. WDAY. Berke rapped with his knuckles on the richly paneled door.

"For a party, they sure keep quiet about it. As dead as a funeral home."

The door opened and music and a babble of voices blasted into the corridor. A tanned figure in a tan shirt with the long pointed collar draped over the loud plaid sport coat smiled at them. He was a little drunk.

"It's open house and to the victors belong the spoils. Come on in and have a snort with Mike Reynard. Who are you?"

Berke said, "I'm Di Berke, of the *Journal*. This is my wife, Gail. We came—"

Reynard stuck out his hand and took Gail's arm. "I like your wife, Berke. Why don't you go get lost in the Collyer mansion? Come back in about two years." He smiled and his forty-year-old face lighted up with an engaging smile.

His other hand took Di's arm. "Come on in," he said, "you're welcome. I'm too old to be a wolf and too young to be a saint. I know why you're here. You want to interview Honey. Nobody wants to interview poor old Mike Reynard. I broke into radio in Detroit twenty years back and now I'm just a broken-down radio emcee and a victory bartender."

Reynard stooped to the floor and picked up a narrow, much-folded piece of paper off the thick carpet. He closed the door, after inserting the paper over the night bolt in the edge of the door. "These doors can't be opened from the outside except with a key. That paper will hold the night bolt back so if we have any more visitors they can walk right in."

Di said, "That's a funny kind of a lock to have on a radio station, chum."

Reynard said, "This is a hotel suite we took over. And this door is wide open all day so the funny lock don't bother us." He waved his hand with a drunken twist. "Come on to the inner sanctum and meet the folks."

He led the way past the engineer's closed-in glass room, filled with dials and turntables and such.

He said, "There ain't nobody here but us chickens. We went off the air at eight with the Crime Buster. Everything's locked up but the big studio."

They moved past a gleaming chromium turntable set against the outside wall of the engineer's room. A record was whirling around and muted music blew softly from concealed loudspeakers, "There'll Be a Hot Time in the Old Town Tonight."

Next was the big central studio, with the walls heavily draped and indirectly lighted from the edges of the ceiling. Overstuffed leather furniture was tastefully arranged and all microphones and radio equipment had been pushed into corners out of the way.

In one corner was a miniature bar and Reynard headed for it. "What'll you have to wet your whistle? Maybe I can make it."

Di said, "Old-fashioned. A Tom Collins for Gail."

A curvaceous blonde with her sheer-stockinged legs crossed carelessly was perched on top of the tiny bar. She had a lot of muscles, but they were nice muscles. No wonder the elevator boy had uttered the wolf whistle. The blonde ignored Gail and smiled provocatively at Di.

"Hi, Red!" she said. "Pull up a stool and name your poison. I'm Honey Hendrix, of Detroit. I never miss the head pin."

Reynard chided her. "Quiet, sis. Wait'll I introduce 'em. Di Berke, sports editor of the *Journal,* and his wife, Gail. She takes pix."

A SIXTY-YEAR-OLD, pasty-faced man in a pencil stripe blue suit that seemed too big for his scrawny frame came into the room. He had a frown on his face and his eyes were a smoldering blur in under his gray bushy brows that matched his thinning hair. He glared at a buxom woman in a low-necked gown sitting on the divan alone.

"Are you coming or not?" he growled.

Reynard said, trying to break the tension, "The guy that just came back is Dan McGuire. He's the political boss of the county and corporation counsel for Dave Nance."

McGuire was slightly drunk. "Not any more," he said, bitterly. "I have been for twenty years. But now he's kicked me off like an old shoe." He turned to the buxom woman, twenty years his junior. "Are you coming or not?"

Reynard still sought to ease the tension. "The amazing Amazon is Mrs. Dan McGuire. Rosie, to you. Best-looking six-foot dame in town. Used to be the best hoofer in the front line at the Gaiety before she married Dan."

Rose McGuire looked at her husband with bored, dull eyes. A raw humor was in her eyes. "That was the big mistake of my life."

Then she transferred her gaze to Reynard.

"Shut up! You talk too much, Mike."

Dan McGuire fastened his eyes on his wife and then turned away and walked away toward the outer door.

"Stay here and make a fool of yourself over Nance," he said. "Finish that drink and then we're getting out of here." He sat down sullenly on the edge of a chair.

Reynard ignored the flare-up. He waved his hand to encompass a trio of men who had moved their chairs into a tight circle in the middle of the room. "The three commissioners are talking politics—Joe Gansweg, Bill Fields, and Fred Lauman."

The three grunted acknowledgments and went back to their discussion.

Di grinned as he accepted two glasses from Reynard and then handed Gail's to her.

"Reynard," he asked, "how can you have a victory celebration without the Mayor? Where's he?"

"He's here. He didn't know there'd be ladies so I carted him off to the shower room so he could pretty up. He'll be back in a minute."

Gail moved to Honey Hendrix, still perched on the bar.

"I'd like some pictures, if you don't

mind. My husband wants a feature for the sport page."

Hendrix said, "Maybe I'd better get my bowling ball."

Di answered, grinning at Gail's pout. "You don't need a bowling ball, Honey. Gail will snap you as is. Cheesecake's always good."

Gail focused her four-by-five and a flash bulb popped. Honey moved to get down off the bar.

Gail said, needling her, "One more, please. Maybe there was too much exposure."

Honey said, "Remind me to kill you some time."

REYNARD had moved across to the turntable and set the needle back in the groove.

"There'll Be a Hot Time in the Old Town Tonight" started over again as Gail's second flash bulb popped.

Then a sharp roar boomed loudly over the musical background. Reynard hastily brushed his hand over a switch panel on the side of the engineer's booth. The music stopped.

It was dead quiet. And then Reynard's voice spat words that were tight, brittle, tense:

"That sounded like a gun! From the shower room!"

He grabbed a key from the pocket of his sport coat and ran across the carpet toward a hall door. He jerked it open and slammed out into the hall. Di Berke was at his heels. Raynard slipped a key into the door directly across the hall and darted into the shower room. Di leaped after him.

The damp smell of hissing hot water and another smell that Di couldn't define hit his nostrils. His eyes flitted over a pile of man's clothing lying disordered on a low bench in front of a long line of shower stalls. Shoes and socks were on the floor.

Then he saw a naked body crumpled up on the floor of the first shower. Boiling hot water drove downward on the bare flesh, making the skin red and blistered looking. The naked man's hand was outstretched on the dry floor outside the shower stall. In the hand was a forty-five revolver.

Reynard's eyes were bulging with terror. His voice shook. "The Mayor! He's killed himself!"

DI LEANED carefully inside the shower stall and twisted the water control. The hissing stopped. The steam evaporated and left the room muggy and silent as death. He turned to Reynard.

"Keep the others out of here!" he said. "This is a job for the police."

He ran back into the central studio. In the deadly quiet he said, "The victory celebration is over. Mayor David Nance is dead! There's a forty-five slug in his heart."

Rose McGuire's face went white except for burning spots on her high cheek bones. Her lips were stiff. "Murder?"

Her eyes went to her husband's sullen face, as if she were probing the thoughts in his brain.

"What made you say murder?" asked Di. "So far it looks like suicide."

He took Gail's camera. "Nance is as naked as a jaybird and cooked well done with boiling water. I'll get a picture and then I'll phone our exclusive to the *Journal*. After that we'll let Homicide in on it."

Dan McGuire's eyes were hard and his voice had a raw edge to it. "Why Homicide? If he killed himself?"

"I said it looked like suicide. But maybe it isn't. In the last half hour I've remembered that a lot of people would probably enjoy seeing Dave Nance dead. Including you."

McGuire's eyes were pin points of rage, but he was a lawyer and he held his temper down. He picked up his hat.

"Come on, Rose," he said to his wife, "I don't want to get mixed up in this. It's unfavorable publicity."

Rose paused. Then she said, putting a strange emphasis on her first word, "I'm still young enough to want to see what goes on. Go ahead, if you want. I'm staying here."

Di pushed McGuire back in his chair. "Unfavorable or not, McGuire, you're sticking around till the cops come. They'll do the deciding between suicide and murder. Guys like Dave Nance who've just been reelected mayor don't usually commit suicide. My vote's for murder."

CHAPTER II

A Strip of Tape

DETECTIVES from the Homicide Bureau had taken charge and, as usual, Lieutenant Fleming Morf was throwing his weight around. This irritated Dwight Berke.

Di said, "The way you strut in on a case, Morf, you ought to have somebody play a fanfare."

Detective Lieutenant Fleming Morf grunted. "I'll run this show from now on, pencil-pusher. Keep out from under foot." He posted two of his stooges in the hall outside the shower room and then inclined his round, crew hair cut skull toward Di and Reynard. "Show me what happened."

Di watched while Morf studied the naked body on the floor of the shower room and then bent over to look at the forty-five in the dead hand.

Morf growled through his heavy lips as he lighted a cigarette and blew heavy smoke through his nostrils.

"Who found the stiff?"

Di said, "You might say we both did. We heard a shot back in the studio and Reynard grabbed a key out of his pocket and came a-running. We found him just like he is now, except that the water was running and it was boiling hot. I turned it off."

Morf grunted. "Reynard, how come you got a key to the shower room? It ain't part of the radio station, is it?"

"No. It's provided by the hotel as a sort of dressing room for the cast when anybody puts on a stage show on the auditorium stage on the floor below. There's a stairway at the end of the hall that leads down to the stage."

"How come you got a key?"

"The hotel manager gave me one. The radio station has no shower facilities. I use it occasionally. I imagine some of the hotel guests on this floor might have keys, too."

"You brought Nance in here?"

"Yeah. We were having a victory celebration over his reelection as mayor. It was supposed to be a stag, but my sister came in and so did Mrs. McGuire. Nance wanted to freshen up a bit, so I brought him into the shower room and then went back to the others."

Morf said, "The lock on that door? You have to have a key to get in?"

"Yeah. Nobody could get in here without a key."

Morf pointed across the room to the east wall. "Where does that door lead to?" Without waiting for an answer he strode across the floor and jerked it open.

A tastefully furnished living room, with overstuffed leather furniture dominating, met his gaze. On a glass-topped coffee table in front of a huge leather divan was a litter of dirty glasses, an empty whisky bottle and a huge bottle of white soda, half full, lying on its side.

Reynard pointed to a bare corner of the room. "There ought to be a piece of furniture there. A chair or something. Looks empty."

Berke walked in from the shower room. He grinned at the sour-faced detective. "What do you think, Big Shot? Still voting for suicide?"

"What else? He had a gun in his hand. He ain't been dead long. And nobody could get in the room without a key."

Di said, "The guy was in boiling water when we found him. How can you tell how long he's been dead?"

Morf said, sullenly, "If that boiling water was on him for long, it'd wash out the wound and take the powder marks off his gun hand."

Di Berke shook his head. "Naw. His gun hand wasn't in the water at all. If he really killed himself, a nitrate test on his gun hand will tell the story."

"You still raving about murder?"

"Could be. Plenty of guys hated Nance. And he just got himself reelected mayor yesterday. Today'd be a devil of a time for him to commit suicide."

"You and Reynard got here a minute after the shot was fired. Two minutes at the most."

Di said, "There's a fire-escape outside the shower room window. Somebody could have shot him and got away down the fire-escape. One thing I'm sure of: this is the funniest case I ever run in to. I took a gander at Nance's clothes.

Shoes, socks, shirt, undershirt, pants, tie, vest and coat."

"So what?"

"No shorts. You think our mayor's been in the habit of going without shorts? Walking raw?"

"Are you dotty? Nobody killed Nance to steal his shorts."

"Just the same, they're gone. Or else he walked around raw."

A SOFT rap sounded on the hall door. Morf held his hand up for silence and moved across the carpet. He jerked the door open violently. Then he growled:

"What do you want, Pop?"

"Pop" was a gaunt, wizened man in faded and patched coveralls that fell in bunches around his ankles and dragged on the carpet, hiding his extremely small shoes. His face was lined and tan as cheap leather and his eyes had a bird-like quality, nervous and quick.

On his gray hair was a striped cap such as railroad brakemen wear. He wore it at such a rakish angle on his sixty-year-old head that Di thought he resembled a soft-ball player. Behind the old-timer, on the floor of the hall, was a huge, brown leather overstuffed chair. And the queer smell of leather wafted into the room.

The old man said, "I'm Ira Jarvis. I'm the new upholsterer for the hotel. I've been here three days. I fixed the springs in the chair seat. I brought it back."

Morf growled. "At ten o'clock at night? Funny hours you keep."

Jarvis smiled. "Hours? Hours don't mean anything when you've lived as long as I hav· I pass plenty of time in forgetfulness. I live in a room the hotel gives me. I get my meals free and a good salary. I work when I please. Many times when I can't sleep, I work."

Di said, "You got a key to this room?"

Jarvis nodded. "Yes, sir. I have a pass key which will open every room in this hotel."

"Why didn't you use it now?"

The weathered hands spread wide. "I do not like to risk embarrassing guests of the hotel." His bird-like eyes flicked over the litter of drinking materials on the coffee table.

"Does your pass key open the shower room next door?"

"Yes, sir, it does. It opens every room in this hotel."

"Do you know who occupies this room?"

"I don't know, sir. I got a notice this morning that a chair needed repairing. All I ever have is the room number."

Morf said, "Let's see if that pass key of yours will unlock the connecting door to the shower room."

Jarvis walked to the door that led to the shower room. He fished a screw-driver out of his pocket and laid it on top of the writing desk by the door. He took a brass key out of the pocket and turned it in the lock of the door and jerked it open.

Di moved quickly across the room and picked up a dirty strip of adhesive tape that was lying near Jarvis' screwdriver.

Morf glowered at him. "Now what, Nosey?"

Di took the strip of tape and pressed the sticky side over the round end of the bolt in the edge of the door, squeezing it tightly to the wood. He closed the door. Then he jerked it open.

"By putting that tape over the bolt you can open the door whenever you want," Di said. "The tape makes it possible to keep the bolt from sliding home. Whoever has this room could have used that tape to enter that room."

Reynard had an odd look of concern on his mobile face. "That sort of puts me on the spot. I used a much-folded sheet of paper to do the same trick on our radio studio door. You saw me do it when I let you in. I could have taken Nance into the shower room, stuck a paper in the door to keep the bolt from sliding home. Then I could have got back in the room without a key—and shot him."

Di grinned. "I don't think you're on the spot. Half a dozen people, including me, can swear that you were in the studio with us when the shot was fired."

Morf grunted. "Let's quit beatin' our gums." He went to the phone and called the room clerk and asked the name of the occupant of Room 1018.

He listened for a long moment and then came back to grin wisely at Di and Reynard. "I'll have the boys throw out a drag. That little strip of adhesive tape might hang the guy that lives in this room. God knows he had reason enough to hate Dave Nance."

Di said, "Whose room is this?"

"Blair Summers'," Morf said. "The defeated candidate for mayor."

Di remembered and his brain was snagged with the possible tie-up. "When Gail and I got out of the elevator a little while ago we met Ted Duffy. He was Summers' campaign manager and his booster on the *Banner*. I thought he was soused—and I guess he had been drinking. But I know now that he was scared to death, too. Better pick him up. And Luke Street, also. The three of them were pals."

HE WAVED at the litter of glasses and bottles on the coffee table. "Maybe the three defeated musketeers were drowning their sorrows and decided to bump off the cause of it all."

Morf could smell a solution right around the corner and he wanted to hog it. "Quit telling me what to do, Berke. I can work this thing out without any help from amateurs."

Di wanted to smash his fist into Morf's button nose but he controlled the urge and stormed out of the room. He joined the jabbering, excited group in the central studio. Morf followed him like an avenging angel.

The detective glared at Mike Reynard. "I'm gonna leave one of my boys in charge here. We'll slap a seal on the outside door."

Reynard fumed. "You can't do that. We go on the air at six o'clock tomorrow morning."

"Not tomorrow, you don't. This station stays sealed till I say the word. I don't want an army of nitwits in here leaving fingerprints all over the joint. All of you get out of here now. At nine o'clock tomorrow morning I want to see all of you in my office at the City Hall. By that time we'll know whether the nitrate test on Nance's gun hand is positive or negative. Then we'll know whether it's suicide or murder."

Honey Hendrix said, "Surely not me, Inspector." She crossed her legs with an obvious pride in their sheer beauty.

Morf grunted and lighted a cigarette. "I'm not an inspector. I'm just a lieutenant. And I've seen legs before. I don't want to see them at nine o'clock tomorrow. But I do want to see you. You better be there."

One of Morf's detectives came in. He had something bulky wrapped up in a white sheet that looked like a housewife's bundle of laundry.

"Boss," he said, "I got the gun and all of Nance's clothes in here. The coroner's putting the body in a basket to haul it away."

Morf said, "Take the stuff to the crime lab. Check the gun for prints and check our permit list to see if you can find out if Nance owned it. Have his hand given the nitrate test. Find out from the coroner when the inquest will be held. I'm sealing up this joint and the shower room. Tell Gregg to stick around and keep his eyes open till further notice."

Di and Gail left the hotel and went back to the *Journal* office.

Gail said, "Do you really think Duffy or Summers or Street could have killed Nance? Probably they hated him, but that kind of reaction to a political beating went out with bustles."

"And nickel beers. We don't know that anybody killed Nance. Maybe it was suicide. But I'm still voting for murder. I'm going to make a long distance phone call. To the *Detroit Leader*. I'm going to see what I can dig up about Dave Nance and Mike Reynard and Honey Hendrix. Dave Nance was legal counsel for an auto company there before he came to town nine years ago and got himself elected mayor. I think it's kind of unusual that all three of them got started in Detroit. Maybe it means something."

CHAPTER III

DENIALS

AT FIVE minutes before nine the next morning Di and Gail walked into Fleming Morf's office in the City Hall.

"What a bust of a reporter you are," Morf said. "You're the last one here. Go in the next room and wait with the rest. I'm talkin' to 'em one at a time."

Di said, "I got a fresh slant on this thing. Want to hear it?"

"I don't need help, Pencil-pusher. I got this case all buttoned up."

Gail put in, "I. I. I. You overwork that word, Sherlock."

Morf only glared.

Di said, "Take it easy, Big Shot. If you got it buttoned up, like you say, I can do you some good in the *Journal*. We'll have an acting mayor and maybe you can build yourself up to inspector."

Morf's eyes wavered and then his jaw jutted out. "Sit over there, then, and don't butt in."

He signaled to a uniformed cop who guarded an inner door. "Bring in Blair Summers."

The cop went out and came back with a haggard, unshaven hulk of a man in a rumpled blue suit that looked like he'd bedded down on a cattle range in it. The collar of his white shirt was minus a button and the knot of his four-in-hand was pulled awry under the points. His eyes were bloodshot and he licked his lips with a nervous tongue. Di recognized him as Blair Summers, the defeated candidate for mayor.

Summers sat down in a chair, nervous. Morf opened a drawer in his desk and pulled out a forty-five revolver. He handed it to Summers.

"It's not loaded, so don't get any ideas. Ever see that before?"

Summers held the gun but he didn't pay much attention to it. "I don't know. Most guns look alike to me."

Morf said, "A slug from that gun killed Dave Nance."

Summers' tongue licked his lips. His bloodshot eyes couldn't meet Morf's relentless stare. "The paper said he shot himself," Summers said.

Di broke in. "I didn't write that he shot himself. I wrote that it looked like suicide."

Morf said, "Berke, I told you to keep your trap shut."

He turned back to Summers. "We know now that Nance didn't shoot himself. The crime lab made a nitrate test on Nance's gun hand and it turned out negative. Nance didn't fire that gun. Somebody else did. And that makes it murder."

Summers' voice was so low they could hardly hear it. "The paper said his body was in boiling water from the shower. The water could have washed away the powder marks, couldn't it?"

"No. His gun hand was outside the shower. It wasn't even wet." Morf clamped his teeth together like he was biting an alibi in half. "He was murdered."

Summers said, "So what? So what? So what?" His voice was low and repeated his words like a faulty phonograph record. He couldn't seem to say anything else with his stiff lips. "So what?"

Morf took the gun out of Summers' clumsy grip. "We checked the serial number on this gun, Summers. You had a permit for it. It's your gun. We know that Nance was murdered and we know he was murdered with your gun."

Summers' eyes wavered crazily. His tongue licked his lips.

The detective said, cruelly, "Start talking."

Berke felt sorry for the defeated mayoralty candidate. Summers went all to pieces. He didn't answer Morf's blast. His eyes rolled in their shadowed sockets; his face muscles contorted as if in agony. His shaking hands went to his lips and then he dropped his head. Sobs shook him. His entire body trembled with his sobbing and the quality of pathos was echoed in the sound. He made no effort to stem his crying. He was sobbing like a heartbroken child, unashamed.

Di said, sympathetically. "Tell your version, Summers. We're listening."

Morf grunted, "Confess, Summers, or we'll slug it out of you! We got ways of getting the truth out of killers. Your room was next to the shower room. Nance was killed with your gun. Come clean."

Summers raised his head. Tears streaked his haggard face. And then fire replaced the dull gleam in his eyes.

"Morf," he said clearly and distinctly, "you're a plain thick-skulled fool! I didn't kill Nance. Neither did Duffy and neither did Street. They were with me. We were drinking." He paused and his eyes moved from Morf to Berke and back again. "We were drunk. We were probably in my room when Nance was killed next door. But we didn't even hear a shot."

Berke said, "I saw Ted Duffy getting on the elevator—it was right after Nance was shot. Why did he leave you and Street?"

"I don't know."

THE face of the Homicide detective reddened with anger. He said, "Berke, I've warned you. Keep your trap out of this."

Summers said, desperately. "I didn't do it. None of us could. We couldn't go through a locked door into the shower room."

Morf grunted triumphantly. "I found out from the hotel that you had a key. And I know all about that strip of adhesive tape we found on your desk by the shower room door. We know how it can be used to hold the bolt down so it won't lock."

Summers' sobs had stopped and his jaw set. "I'm not saying one more word until I talk to my lawyer."

Berke said, "Summers, did you and Duffy and Street go to your room together?"

Summers hesitated and his face relaxed slightly. "Yes, it was somewhere around nine o'clock."

"Did you all leave your room together?"

"No. Duffy stayed for one drink, then he left. Street and I had another drink. Then we left, too."

"You heard no shot from the shower room?"

"So help me God. . . . No."

"But that is your gun?"

"Yes. I kept it in the drawer of my desk. It's my gun, all right, but I didn't kill Nance."

Berke said, "Thanks."

Morf waved to the cop. "Cool him off in a cell. He'll talk, lawyer or no lawyer."

Luke Street was the next one brought in. He was tall and bulky of body in a brown suit that was tight across his enormous shoulders. His hair was a stubbly red and he had a red stubble on his fat cheeks. He had a bulbous nose and thick lips and pale blue eyes.

Morf said, suddenly, "Why did you kill Dave Nance?"

Street stared at him, a raw humor in his eyes. "Are you goofy?"

"You had motive enough to kill him."

"Sure. I've been working for the Street Department for twenty-three years, ten of them as superintendent of the department. In two more years I'd gone on pension at half pay. Nance fired me the minute he knew he was reelected. I hated his insides, but I didn't kill him."

Morf said, "Why—"

"Hold it, Morf," Street said, "I told you all I'm going to tell. I didn't kill Nance and you got no right to hold me. You can shoot off at your big mouth till you're blue in the face. I'm not doing any more talking." He clamped his jaws shut.

Ted Duffy was next. He still had on the tweed suit and it bore no trace of a crease. His collar was rumpled, his cuffs were dirty and his face was haggard and drawn. Beard stubbled his face. His eyes were bloodshot and wavering.

Morf tried the same old tactics of surprise. "Why did you kill Dave Nance?"

"I didn't," Duffy said. "He was already dead when I saw him."

"What?" Morf's exclamation was a shrill scream. "You saw him?"

"Yes. I'll tell you the whole thing. Me and Summers and Street went up to Blair's room for a drink. It was the first time I'd ever been in the room. We had a drink. I started looking for the bathroom. I opened the door of the shower room, thinking it was the bathroom. A piece of adhesive tape was on the floor. I picked it up and laid it on the desk. I didn't know it at the time, but that tape must have been stuck over the door bolt to keep it from sliding home. I went into the shower room. I heard water running and the hiss of steam. Then I saw the body on the floor under the shower and I saw the gun."

Morf prompted him. "Go on."

Duffy finished. "I didn't even know who it was. I didn't care. I went back into Summers' room. I made up an excuse, and got out of there. I didn't want to get mixed up in a murder."

Di broke in. "How'd you know it was murder, Duffy?"

Duffy was unruffled. "I didn't. I

didn't even know then who the dead guy was. But I got sense enough to know that the cops don't hold wholesale inquisitions about a simple suicide."

Morf motioned to the cop. "Hold this guy."

Duffy said, "You can't hold me. I told you the truth."

Morf grinned cagily. "Maybe so. But you might turn out to be a key witness and we don't want to take a chance of having you bumped off."

DAN McGUIRE came in with a surly grimace on his pasty face and a chip on his shoulder. "You got nothing on me, Morf, and you know it. Don't ask me questions or I'll make a prize fool of you."

Morf bridled. "I don't scare easy, McGuire. You used to be cock of the walk in politics in this burg but you're small potatoes now. You can't hurt me. I want answers."

McGuire said, "Bushwah."

"When your wife heard the news about Nance's death she gave you a very funny look, and she was the first to jump at the conclusion that Nance had been murdered. Why?"

McGuire said, "Ask her."

"Nance kicked you out as corporation counsel, a job you'd held since Strongheart was a pup."

"What of it?"

"Rumor has it your wife was pretty well sold on Dave Nance. I've seen her at night spots with Dave myself. Revenge against him for kicking you out of your job and jealousy make good motives for murder."

"So I've heard," McGuire sneered. His attitude made it plain that he was going to be difficult. Morf realized it promptly.

He motioned to the cop.

"Take him out of here. He's smart—we'll treat him that way. Later."

Morf then questioned Mike Reynard, Honey Hendrix, Rose McGuire, and the three commissioners, Joe Gansweg, Bill Fields and Fred Lauman. Their stories were clear and concise and coincided with the happenings in the radio studio just previous to the discovery of Nance's death. Di tried to break in while Morf was questioning Mike Reynard and Honey Hendrix but the detective again stormed against his interference.

CHAPTER IV

ANOTHER CORPSE

WHEN the series of interviews was over Morf told the cop, "Hold Summers and Duffy for a while. Turn the rest of them loose. Tell 'em not to leave town."

Di said, "Big Shot, I made a telephone call last night and I had a pal on the *Detroit Leader* do a little digging in the *Leader's* morgue. I came up with an angle."

Morf's lips curled. "Still playing Sherlock, eh? What you or your pal can dig out of newspaper files wouldn't have no bearing on Nance's murder."

Di was stubborn. "If I had any brains, I'd let you blunder your way right out of your job. But I don't like murder enough to hold out on you. Listen, you big-headed flat-foot. Dave Nance, Mike Reynard, and Honey Hendrix all got started in Detroit. Don't that ring a bell in that thick skull of yours?"

"A lot of things got started in Detroit. Henry Ford, Joe Louis and bubble gum." Morf chuckled at the quip.

"Listen, chump. Dave Nance was a lawyer back in Detroit in his early days before he got to be a counsel for an auto company. He was in partnership with an educated Swede by the name of Gunnar Olafson. They got caught in a shady deal. Nance beat the rap, but the law gave Olafson ten years in the penitentiary. Rumors at the time said the Swede had been framed to take the rap alone, while Nance went free."

Morf lighted a cigarette and blew smoke through his button nose. Then he yawned as if bored. "I know all that, amateur. I'm three blocks ahead of you and going down hill. We checked on him last night with Detroit police. Olafson went to the pen, like you say. He hated Nance, let's say, and he wanted to get loose and get even. So he framed a prison break with a pal. And he would of made it, only he got himself killed under the wheels of a freight train three years ago. Olafson is dead. The body was cut up pretty badly, but there wasn't a doubt about it being Olafson on account of his size five shoes. So your revenge motive died right along with Olafson, under the wheels of that freight!"

Di said, "I didn't think human skulls were made of concrete. Did it ever occur to you, wise guy, that although Mike Reynard and Honey Hendrix are brother and sister and she's never been married, their last names are not alike?"

"So what? The gal's a bowler. The guy's a radio emcee. Maybe one of them wanted a classier handle. That Reynard's a fox."

"That's right," Di grinned. "Olafson wouldn't sound too good over a microphone and Olafson is a little too long for a one-column bowling score."

DEAD silence. Then Morf threw his cigarette away. "Did you say Olafson?"

Di said, "I said Olafson. I'm trying to get it through your thick skull that Honey Hendrix and Mike Reynard are Gunnar Olafson's kids. Does that sound like the revenge motive is dead?"

Morf's face reddened with rage. "Why in the devil didn't you say so before?"

"You wouldn't let me. You said you had this case all buttoned up. You wouldn't let me get a word in edgeways."

Morf jumped out of his chair and moved to the door and yelled at one of his detectives. "Bring the car around in front. We're going over to WDAY. Pronto."

Morf's aide, "Dutch" Beggs, was sitting in a chair propped up against the door to WDAY. Mike Reynard was at the end of the corridor when Di, Gail and Morf barged out of the elevator and made Beggs lose his balance and tumble out of the chair flat on the carpet.

Morf said, "Bust the seal, Beggs. We're opening up."

Reynard came down the hall quickly. Morf saw him and growled. "You ain't back on the air just yet but we want to talk to you. Come on in."

Di and Gail followed them into the studio. Reynard hit a couple of light switches and radiance flooded the room. As they passed the enclosed glass engineer's room, Morf tried the knob.

"Reynard," he said, "you got a key. Open it up."

Reynard took a key out of his pocket and unlocked the door. He started to walk inside.

"Stay out of there," Morf said.

Reynard gave an odd shrug and followed the group past the turntable outside of the engineer's room and into the big central studio. Nothing had been changed. It was just the same as it had been on the previous evening.

Morf said to Reynard, "Where were you standing when you heard the shot last night?"

Reynard hesitated, and his face paled. "Here by the outside turntable," he said. "I had just turned the switch on a record that we were playing."

Di moved across and looked at the record. "Same tune. There'll Be a Hot Time in the Old Town Tonight." Then inspiration nicked his brain. "Say, how could we hear in here a shot fired in the shower room. I thought radio studios were soundproofed."

Morf had a supercilious grin on his thick features. "You're slow, genius. What do you think I've been driving at? That shot you all heard wasn't from the shower room. It was a sound effect built right into that record on the turntable." He menaced Reynard with hard eyes. "Make with the switches, sonny boy."

Reynard set the needle on the record and flipped a switch on the panel and a slight scratching started and then the peppy strains issued from a hidden speaker. Morf listened until the record had finished.

Reynard grinned. "Wise guy! You didn't hear a shot, did you?"

Morf grunted and shook his head. He'd missed the head pin again.

Di was looking at the switch panel. He glanced at Reynard. "What does this switch turn on? The one next to the one for the outside turntable that you just used?"

Reynard pointed to a similar turntable inside the engineer's room. "We can turn that one on from out here if we want to."

Di smiled. "Turn it on. Maybe we'll hear something."

Reynard said, "It won't play. The

needle ain't on the platter."

Di looked through the glass. "It is. Wait. I'll move it back to the first grooves." He went into the engineer's room and moved the needle back to the edge of the cuts. He came out.

Morf said, "Turn on the song, Reynard."

Reynard flipped the switch that controlled the outside turntable. The music of: "There'll Be a Hot Time in the Old Town Tonight" floated through the room. Morf moved forward quickly and flipped the switch to the turntable in the engineer's room.

The sharp crack of a pistol shot echoed through the room from the hidden speaker.

MORF flipped the switches and his eyes bored into Reynard's face. "You had a nifty trick, Reynard, but it didn't work. I'm taking you in for the killing of Dave Nance."

Reynard said, "You're crazy!"

"Yeah? How does this sound? You took Nance to the shower room. He got his clothes off and got under the shower. You shot him. Then you came back here and started that record. You thought you'd made yourself a perfect alibi. You figured nobody would suspect you of murder when you were here in the studio with a half dozen people when the shot was heard. We caught up with you."

Reynard was oddly calm and Di had to admire him. Reynard said, "I had no reason to kill Nance and I didn't kill him."

"No reason?" asked Di. "Nance let your father take a ten year rap in the Michigan penitentiary. A term in prison, and then he was killed right after a prison break. You had plenty of reason to kill Nance, all right."

"Have it your way. But I didn't kill him." Reynard angrily flipped the switch that controlled the turntable in the engineer's room.

Out of the speaker came the spine chilling sound of the rattle of machine-gun bullets, the screech of crazily skidding tires, the squeal of brakes and the slam-bang crash of automobiles in head-on collision. An excited, high-pitched voice screamed:

"Listen to the thrilling adventures of Duke Savage, the Crime Buster. As we take up our story tonight, Duke Savage is lying unconscious at the foot of the cliff. The evil lawyer, Silas Dawson—"

Reynard flipped the switch and the voice died. "That's the transcription to Crime Buster. That's our sign-off program at seven forty-five each night. The engineer must have left the needle down on the platter. I was a little drunk last night. I bumped both switches and both records played."

Morf said, disgruntled. "We'll check on that fairy tale, Reynard."

He grunted at Di as the phone rang. "Take it, Berke. Tell 'em I'm not here."

Di picked up the phone. He said hello and listened for a moment and then hung up. He frowned at Morf.

"That was the room clerk. He's got a job for you."

"Tell him to go chase himself. Tell him I'm busy."

"You'll be busy, all right. One of the maids went into a guest's room to make up the bed. The guest won't be needing a bed any more. A lady has been murdered."

Morf's mouth dropped open. "What lady?"

Di said, "Mrs. Dan McGuire!"

CHAPTER V

CLOSED CASE

HURRYING to a phone, Di called Gail at the *Journal* and she came arunning with her four-by-five to snap a picture of the new body in Room 723. Rose McGuire was lying face up on an overstuffed leather divan. She might have been sleeping. Her head was resting on a crocheted piece that bore the initials D. McG. Directly above her on the wall was a framed sampler, obviously her own needlework, that bore the legend, "God Bless Our Home." But her throat bore red bruises from the hands that had strangled her life away.

Di said to Morf, "You can't hang this one on Reynard. He was in your office from nine o'clock on. This dame ain't been dead more than an hour. You can't hang it on Summers or Duffy. They're in the jail house."

Morf grunted. "We won't have to hang it on anybody but Dan McGuire. He's flew the coop. We been hunting him since last night. He ain't been to his office. I got a dragnet out."

"Why would McGuire kill his own wife?"

Morf lighted a cigarette. "It all adds up. McGuire came late to Reynard's party. He could of gone to the shower room and killed Nance and then come to the party. The minute Mrs. McGuire heard that Nance was dead she gave her husband that funny look and jumped at murder. You said so yourself. I figure McGuire killed Nance because Dave kicked him out of his job as corporation counsel and maybe because Nance was running around with his wife."

"If McGuire killed Nance for running around with his wife, why would he kill his wife after Nance was out of the way? And you forget the fact that Nance was killed with Blair Summers' gun."

"We'll straighten that out okay. I figure McGuire killed Nance and then killed the dame because she was going to tell what she knew." He blew smoke through his nose. "This case is all buttoned up. When we pick up Dan McGuire we got the double killer."

Di gave a last look around the room and then he grinned at his wife. "Come on, baby, we are going to rent a room."

Twenty minutes later they were in Room 526 and the bellhop took Di's half dollar and grinned. "How you gonna stay six months with no baggage, chum?"

Di said, "It'll come. Thanks. And good-by."

After the door closed behind the bellhop, Gail sat down on the overstuffed leather divan and looked at her husband. "I'd like to ask the same thing, darling. We've got a home of our own. Why'd you tell that room clerk we wanted a room for six months?"

"So we'd be permanent residents, baby. We got a right to insist on first-class furniture."

"I don't know what you're talking about."

Di took a pocket-knife out of his pocket and opened a blade. He jabbed the point of the sharp steel into a seam of one of the leather cushions on the davenport and then ripped a long slash in the thick leather. He turned the cushion over and jammed the blade into the cushion again. He ripped the fabric wide so the padding was exposed.

He grinned at his wife. "Now, baby, you get on the phone and call the room clerk. You raise the devil about that cushion and tell him you want it fixed pronto or we'll move to another hotel for six months."

"What are you going to do?" Gail's eyes were puzzled.

Di went to the door. "I'll be seeing you in a little while, baby. You do just exactly as I told you." He closed the door and vanished down the hall.

He went up the iron stairway to the ninth floor. He opened the door of a linen closet and stepped inside, pulling the door almost shut behind him. A crack of light enabled him to watch the shadowed corridor without being seen by anybody passing in the hall.

For ten minutes he stood there motionless. His muscles began to ache with the unmoving position in the cramped quarters. And then his ears were turned to the click of a door latch and the noise of a closing door. He saw a shadow flit across the light that seeped into the crack of the door opening and then he saw a dark figure move silently up the carpeted hall toward the passenger elevators.

He waited without moving until he heard the elevator stop and a voice say clearly: "Fifth floor."

He opened the linen closet door and sprang across the hall. He tried the door of the room, knowing already that it had automatically locked. He used a skeleton key expertly, opened the door and walked in. It was almost dark because the one window shade was pulled all the way down to the sill. Di flipped the tumbler light switch at the side of the door with the heel of his hand.

THE room smelled of leather and varnish and a work bench littered with tools was against the south wall of the room. Cans of paint and samples of leather, made up in stapled swatches, were on a central battered and paint smeared rough wooden table. A davenport, of leather, with springs sticking through the cushions, and leather chairs in various stages of repair, stood about the room.

He hurried to a door in the north wall and went through. Again he flicked a light switch. He grinned.

This was what he was looking for. This was where his quarry lived and slept. He closed the door behind him.

A metal bed, stained walnut, was against the west wall where a window should have been. Beside the bed was a tiny table that held a telephone and a hand-carved ash tray in the likeness of Abraham Lincoln. The top of the head was hollowed out. It looked like a homemade job. A chest of drawers was on the north wall. A closet door swung open to reveal clothes hanging inside.

He opened the drawers in the chest and searched them systematically one by one. He knew what he was looking for. He didn't find it.

He moved to the closet. His eyes caught the extremely small shoes lined up neatly on the floor. A tan pair of oxfords and a pair of brown and white summer shoes.

He shoved his right hand in turn into the pockets of the three suits. He rummaged through boxes on the high shelf in the closet. He came out and closed the door. He stood in the middle of the room and looked around, his brow puckered in a frown, disappointment in his eyes.

He started for the door. Then he muttered to himself, "The bed is out. The maid probably makes that up for him every morning. It's got to be the chest or the closet."

A sudden idea snagged his brain. "Maybe it's dust-proof." He crossed to the chest of drawers. He pulled the top drawer clear out. The chest was of dust-proof construction and the drawers were separated by thin plywood. A thin sheet of paper lay on top of the plywood. It was yellow and dry. It was a gummed label that carried the factory number of the furniture and the name of the maker.

Di put the top drawer back and jerked the second one out. And a queer surge of excitement prickled the hair at the back of his neck. On the thin plywood was a soft, shiny splotch of thin silk. He put the drawer on the floor. He picked up the splotch of silk and the expensive material was cool and rich in his trembling hands. He parted the silken folds and embroidered letters stared up at him. D. N.

He dropped the silk in his pocket. He heard a click and his senses clamored a warning to his brain. Too late.

He whirled toward the door into the work room.

"Gail!" he gasped. He stammered in his excitement. "W-where's—" He turned back and fumbled crazily on the table by the bed.

Gail's face was drawn, pale. She didn't answer. She walked into the room, stiffly, her eyes focused on the drawer on the floor.

Di turned and asked, "Where's—"

Then he saw the danger. Ira Jarvis slipped into the room behind her, quietly, not at all excited. He was dressed in the same old coveralls and he wore the same striped cap at the same rakish angle. His face was tan and his skin had the texture of leather and his eyes were flitting like a bird. But he wasn't a meek and kindly man.

He had a gun in his right hand. He had it pointed casually at Di's belt buckle but Di was quite sure he could hit what he shot at; his flat stomach muscles crawled.

Jarvis' eyes moved. His mouth was twisted downward at the corners. He looked at the drawer on the floor.

"You're smarter than I thought. I see you found what you were looking for." It was almost like a question.

Di's mouth was dry and his tongue was stiff. Momentarily he could not speak.

Jarvis said, with a raw humor, "You were cagey. Slashing that divan in Room Five-twenty-six so you could get me up there and out of here long enough to give the place the once-over. I caught on quick. I saw that divan had been slashed with a knife and your wife made the mistake of not hiding that camera of hers. I brought her down here. I caught on quick."

"Not quick enough." Di's voice had sudden power and the sound gushed out of him and bounced off the walls. "They'll slit your pants and shave your skull and then turn on the juice, Jarvis. For the murders of Dave Nance and Rose McGuire."

JARVIS could have been talking about the weather, he was so casual. "I didn't think you'd tumble to it."

"I didn't. Until you killed the dame and I got into her room, and found out she was handy with a needle. Then I figured maybe some of her needlework was on those silk shorts that were missing after Dave Nance was killed."

Jarvis' eyes blinked. "You are cagey. The dame was crazy about Nance. Her husband was too old for her. In my racket I got into a lot of rooms. I found out a lot of dirt about the guests. I found out she embroidered lots of stuff that didn't have her husband's initials on 'em. I took them shorts of Nance's to the dame. Told her I'd show them to her hubby if she didn't kick in with five grand. She grabbed the phone to call the cops. I had to bump her off."

Di said, his voice still booming, "Why'd you kill Dave Nance?"

"Why? Or how?" His bright eyes gleamed. "I went to Summers' room to see if I could bring his repaired chair back. I saw Reynard taking Nance across the hall to the shower room. I went in Summers' room, took his gun out of his desk—I told you I found out a lot of stuff in my racket—opened the shower room door with my key and shot Nance."

"Why?"

"You figure that one out." Jarvis waved his gun at Gail. "Lie down on the floor! Your hubby's going to tie you up. You can stay here a day while I make tracks." He tossed a short length of rope he held in his left hand toward Di.

"Tie her up, smart guy! And don't get funny. I shoot straight."

Di moved around the end of the bed and stooped to pick up the rope. His fingers touched it. But he didn't straighten up. He was poised on the balls of his feet. With one desperate, fluid motion of his muscles he dived forward toward Jarvis, his shoulders a battering ram.

A roar blasted his ears as the gun went off. A hot pain seared across his side. And then he thrilled as his shoulders socked into Jarvis' knees. The gun came down in a vicious swipe and hard metal flicked across his skull.

He twisted sideways, viciously. His quarry screamed in frenzy. Jarvis went down under the shattering tackle, his thin frame bouncing as he hit the floor. The gun flew from his hand.

Di squirmed loose and scrambled to his knees. He drove his fist at a motionless target. He hit the jackpot of Jarvis' jaw. The man groaned and fell back, his eyes closed. He was out, cold.

Gail picked up the gun and gave it to Di with trembling hands.

Suddenly the room was full of men. Fleming Morf and several of his detectives. He had handcuffs ready and he snapped them on Ira Jarvis' wrists. Then he crossed the room to the little table beside the bed.

He took the little Abraham Lincoln ash tray from under the telephone receiver. "Operator wants the receiver back on the hook." His face flushed red as he paid unwilling tribute. "Pretty slick, Berke, putting that ash tray under that telephone receiver so the operator would hear you. She notified me pronto and we came running. I'll remember this."

Di said, "Don't worry, Morf, you can have the glory. I'll take exclusive on the story and pix." He grinned. "Seems to me you had Dan McGuire all tagged for the killings."

Morf said, "We found Dan. He was at the Country Club. He was soused to the gills since last night." His voice was grudging. "I never give the upholsterer a tumble. He was using his trade as a shakedown racket. I guess we was both wrong on the revenge motive."

Di grinned. "The dame was the victim of a shakedown. Nance wasn't. Nance was killed for revenge."

"I don't get it."

"I'll draw you a picture. Where do you think the killer learned the upholstery trade? In the penitentiary. It took him three years to find Nance after he broke out."

Morf's mouth dropped open. "You mean—"

"Yeah. This Ira Jarvis is really Gunnar Olafson."

"Rats! Olafson is dead. He died under that freight train."

"They never had any real proof. Only his little shoes and his clothes. Olafson killed his prison-break pal and put his body on the railroad track, with his own clothes and his own shoes. The cops took it for granted the body was Olafson's on account of the small shoes."

THE killer opened his eyes and groaned. Morf pulled him up off the floor. "Them kids of yours was in on this. Mike Reynard and Honey Hendrix."

Olafson quailed and his voice shook. "They didn't even know I was here. If you got any brains, you'll let it ride that way."

They led Olafson out into the hall, the handcuffs bright on his wrists, and rode down in the elevator to the lobby. As they crossed the Chinese rug in a solid phalanx, Mike Reynard and Honey Hendrix came out of the coffee shop. They stared unbelieving at the man in handcuffs.

Reynard said, "Is he the one?"

Di said, hastily, before Morf could open his mouth, "He's the one. He was playing a blackmail racket. He used his trade to dig up dirt on the hotel guests and then tried to shake them down."

Reynard's voice was raw. His eyes stared. "What's his name?"

Di wet his lips with his tongue. "Ira Jarvis. Know him?"

Reynard shook his head in puzzlement, as if he were trying to remember into the past. Then he shook his head. "It couldn't be. But I've seen him somewhere before. Some time."

Di said, "Could be."

He took Gail's arm hastily and said, softly, "Let's go, baby, we've got a story to write."

New York's Finest

NEW YORK CITY'S Police Commissioner, Arthur W. Wallander, carries as expensive a piece of official jewelry on him as some of the medieval officers of royalty. Costing about $400, and actually belonging to the city, it is a 14 carat gold badge with four platinum stars. The commissioner houses it in a battered black leather case that may once have cost two dollars. Proud to possess it, Commissioner Wallander is prouder that he never has to use it. Each of his 19,000 men know him by sight.

Wallander first saw the gaudy bauble on September 3, 1945, when retiring Commissioner Valentine handed it to him along with the responsibilities of office. Valentine preferred not to lug the quarter pound badge around with him and so he had a miniature made for himself that cost just under $40. Valentine got the big badge from Commissioner James S. Bolan, for whom it was cast in 1933. There is only one like it in the world.

A little more than 100 years ago New York policemen didn't have any badges at all. Their insignia was a leather helmet-like hat which earned them the name "leatherheads." Nor were they happy about having to varnish these leather head covers twice a year tho it did make them look better and as stiff as a modern steel helmet. Cops then also carried a thirty-inch long club, which folks referred to as their walking sticks.

New York city's "Star police" were organized in 1845 under Mayor Havenmeyer. They wore the first of the stars Mark Sennett later made famous. Havenmeyer also fathered the term "New York's finest" about this time in a reëlection speech. He called them the "finest police body in the world."—*Simpson M. Ritter.*

Parry Kaw's only clues are a new fur coat and the girl who modeled it!

The big man plunged into the river

A HIGH HAT for HOMICIDE

by

O. B. MYERS

THE Shir-Lee Shoppe was on Fifty-Third Street, just around the corner from Lexington Avenue. It occupied the ground floor of a remodeled brownstone building. There were apartments upstairs, with a separate entrance. The location, nearer to the Third Avenue El than it was to Park Avenue, was neither one thing nor the other, and had a tendency to display the worse features of both.

There was a thin cluster of loiterers as close to the door as the uniformed cop would let them get. He kept shooing them along about their business with a desultory air. Parry Kaw spoke to him briefly, without opening his coat, and the officer nodded. He rapped, the door opened, and Parry went in.

From the front of the store he could see nothing of the body except the feet, clad in russet high-heeled slippers, which extended just beyond the edge of a light partition dividing the interior, about halfway back. In between there was a great bustle of activity, for Homicide was already in force.

Inspector Draper was established behind a short section of counter, tossing questions at a tall, thin man with a high forehead and loose, nervous lips. A clerk at his elbow made shorthand notes of the replies, which seemed to increase the nervousness of the man being questioned.

The inspector's minions, most of them in plain clothes, trotted back and forth, poking into the racks, the cupboards, the counters, everywhere, occasionally running to their chief to report their finds. Beyond the partition two men knelt on the broadloom rug, and two others leaned to peer over their shoulders. Photographers shifted their tripods from one point to another.

A couple of the detectives nodded to Parry. After several minutes the inspector noticed him, and gave him a half smile.

"Hello, there, Kaw," he greeted. "What the devil is Safe-and-Loft doing way up here?"

Parry made a deprecatory gesture. "It's a robbery, isn't it, Inspector?"

A faintly contemptuous shrug was his reply. "It's murder," said the inspector flatly. "From what I can see, the robbery was just an afterthought, to throw out false clues. We'll probably find the missing coats and suits in some alley, any minute now. Better keep your fingers out of the gears, Kaw, until we're set."

Parry made his nod respectful. "I'll just stand around and listen," he murmured.

FOR nearly an hour he was content to do just that. He was second fiddle here, and knew it. When it was murder, Homicide reigned supreme. The boys on Homicide for that reason were inclined to feel somewhat superior, to consider themselves the elite of the force, pushing Safe-and-Loft and the many other specialists into the background. When they did it with a sneer, Parry could be annoyed.

Merely by using his ears he picked up most of the facts. The shop had been owned and run by a woman named Roszinda Skoviescher, a naturalized Austrian. Since arriving in New York ten years ago, she had used the name of Shirley Leeton, for reasons which, as her brother explained plaintively, were obvious. There had been no intent to evade or confuse the law, unless you included Gestapo persecution under the general heading of the law. She had been in no trouble since reaching the States—none whatever.

"And when did you last see her alive?"

The tall man passed one hand over his thinning hair. Apparently he had already answered this question at least once.

"Last evening, she had dinner with me." He spoke with a slight accent, pronouncing "evening" with three syllables. "At the *Cordon Bleu,* a small French restaurant on West Thirtieth Street. We are finished a little after nine o'clock, perhaps nine-thirty. She left me on the corner of Eighth Avenue; she said she would walk back here to the shop, to put tickets on some new stock."

"Walk? From Thirtieth and Eighth to Fifty-Third and Lexington is a long walk."

"I do not *know* that she walked; that is what she said."

"And what did you do, after she left you?"

"I also walked, but downtown, to my apartment on Sheridan Square. I read a book, then went to bed."

"Did you meet any friends on your walk? Stop to talk with anyone, go in any stores?"

Karel Skoviescher shook his head sadly. Apparently he was aware of the significance of an alibi. "Unfortunately, no. I did not."

The inspector, his eyes narrowing, sat silent for fully a minute. It was easy to guess what he was thinking. If this man before him, after taking leave of his sister, had jumped into a taxi instead of walking downtown, he could easily have reached Fifty-Third Street in time to waylay her in the shop. The inspector's next question betrayed his line of thought.

"Have you a key to this store?"

Karel admitted that he did. "I am not interested in the business—financially, I mean to say. But I came here often. My sister always asked my advice about her affairs, and consulted me about new merchandise. We talked at dinner about the Ritzton coats, for example. She had just gotten a shipment of several dozen. She showed me one, and we discussed the price, and the advertising."

The inspector asked, "What are the Ritzton coats?"

The tall man gestured toward a blank gap in the rack behind him. "The thieves must have taken them—all of them It is a late model, strongly promoted by the manufacturer, and very much in demand. A suede weave, silk lined, and trimmed with fur collar and cuffs. They are the very latest fashion, advertised to retail at one hundred forty-nine dollars, and Roszinda was paying for them eleven hundred dollars a dozen. But wait!"

He pulled open a drawer in the next show-case and fingered through some papers. After a moment he brought out a single sheet advertising leaflet on which was printed a description of the Ritzton coat next to a full-length photograph of an incredibly beautiful brunette wearing one with an air of calculated nonchalance. Both Parry and the inspector eyed the girl's picture appreciatively. After a moment the inspector asked:

"This is not your sister in the illustration, is it?"

"Oh, no! A professional model, I presume."

The inspector winked at Parry. "Too bad! She would add zest to the case, if we could drag her in."

He laid the leaflet aside as the medical examiner came from the rear of the store to make his preliminary report.

"Death caused by a blow on the head," he said. "Bones of the skull crushed inward by a blunt instrument, on the left side, and somewhat to the rear, as if the blow was delivered from behind. No other apparent injuries."

"What time?" asked the inspector.

THE physician frowned faintly. "Between eleven and thirteen hours is as close as I can give it to you now."

"In other words, around ten o'clock last night?"

The doctor nodded. "Only one blow, it seems."

"I beg your pardon, doctor." The murdered woman's brother spoke hesitantly. "Did you say on the left side?" At a nod of assent the brother continued. "That is why only one blow was necessary, even a light one. Her skull was already broken, on that side." In reply to the inspector's look of astonishment he explained, "In Nineteen Thirty-Eight, in Wiener-Neustadt, in the course of a—an interrogation by the Gestapo. She was in the hospital for two months afterward. The doctors repaired it with a fragment of bone from her leg, but she was warned that it would always be fragile."

The inspector looked displeased. The dragging of ancient motivations into the case would not make his task any easier.

He asked, "Who else knew about that?"

"Oh, very few; almost no one. It gave her no trouble, but she did not speak about it to her friends."

The inspector's eyes were grim. "Then anyone who did know it, would know exactly where to strike in order to kill her easily?"

Her brother, seeing where this led, was pale as he countered, "Or a robber, knowing nothing, would strike only hard enough to render her unconscious, but would discover he had killed her."

The inspector shrugged, and turned to the doctor. "Take her out the back way, by the alley, if they've got all their photographs, so the crowd on the sidewalk won't see her."

Parry followed the doctor back to the rear. The body on the floor, reported as 35 years old, looked younger, perhaps because the delicately chiseled features were in complete repose. She had dark hair, cut short and fluffed very full and soft, and her lips, bright red against the chalky pallor of her cheeks, were parted as if about to smile. Only the ugly dark stain on the carpet evidenced the brutal fate which had struck her down.

Parry paused, and sniffed several times. His expression showed he was puzzled. He looked questioningly at the doctor.

"Cuir de Russie," volunteered the doctor. "She went for foreign perfumes, I guess. There's a small flask of it in her handbag." He pointed to the desk top, where the contents of a pocketbook were spread out for inspection. Parry read the inscription on the tiny bottle, sniffed the stopper, and put it down again.

Getting out of the way of two men with a stretcher, he moved toward the back door. This opened on a paved yard, connected to the side street by an alley, which served for trucks to reach the rear entrances of several stores facing on the avenue. A long, black vehicle with a closed body stood there now, waiting.

The door itself had been forced; a photographer was taking pictures of the marred jamb. Parry saw that the paint had been scratched, but the woodwork only slightly dented. This was within the field of his experience. He surmised that the job had been done with a light jimmy, and by a hand that knew exactly how much pressure to apply, and at what point.

Would Karel be an adept jimmy artist? he thought. And if he had a key, why jimmy the door?

Parry strolled again to the front of the shop. The inspector was busy requestioning the elderly saleswoman who had first opened the street door and discovered the body. Karel Skoviescher stood backed up against a showcase, a cigarette between his long, nervous fingers, under the eye of a man in uniform. Parry tried to lessen his tension by asking for a light.

"Do you know how much merchandise was taken?" he asked.

"There has not been time for inventory," was Skoviescher's answer. "But all the coats, as you can see, and some silk underwear from the drawers there. I don't know how much. And the handbags that were in the showcase behind you, the best ones, are gone, too."

"The thieves knew the best stuff when they saw it, eh?"

Karel shrugged. "Apparently, yes."

"You say she brought along one of those Ritzton coats to show you, last night?"

"She wore it." Then he explained quickly. "It was not her habit to wear clothes that were to be sold, later. But it was the easiest way to bring it to me, and she was very careful of it, so that it could be returned to stock, here."

"I see."

PARRY smoked on his cigarette. He was trying to form a picture in his mind of the sequence of events around ten o'clock on the previous evening.

The attractive young business woman, intent on her affairs, returning to her shop to ready up some new stock for the next day's business. Opening the door with her key, switching on perhaps one light in the front. Removing her coat, the new Ritzton, and after a sharp inspection putting it on the rack with the others—all while the thieves, surprised in the midst of their predatory operations, lurked in hiding behind the partition. Then the woman walking, all unheeding, toward the rear, where her desk was, until passing through the opening in the partition, without warning, they killed her.

Yes, the picture fitted, except for her coat.

"You say that every one of the Ritzton coats is gone?"

Karel, who had already answered this question several times, spread his palms. "You can see for yourself."

Parry proceeded to do exactly that. Not content with the empty rack, he looked on all the other racks, opened drawers, peered into closets, investigated the desk, and even got down on hands and knees to look under the showcases. His search was thorough, and when he got through he was sure that there was not a single Ritzton coat in that store.

He perceived—if he could lay hands on it—that he might have here a key to unlock this whole affair. One dozen brand new coats are very much like another dozen; they are unidentifiable;

there is nothing to distinguish one batch from the other. There were several hundred stores in the metropolitan area handling Ritzton coats, and doubtless a score of wholesalers. A searcher could look through their stock for weeks without knowing whether he was looking at stolen goods of legitimate merchandise. That was, as Parry well knew, the great problem with recovery of loot.

But a coat which has been worn was a bird of another feather. Even though it had been worn but once, there was a chance of its carrying some mark of that wearing. The proceeds of a robbery, before being put back in circulation through a fence, would of course have the pockets searched and the labels removed or changed. But if, as Parry suspected, these thieves had simply scooped up *all* of the Ritzton garments without knowing that one of them had been worn, that chance existed. The trick was to ferret it out, and seize it.

There was also a possibility, he reflected, that the robbers had departed wholly unaware that they had committed murder. They had struck to silence, not to kill, and in their eagerness to be gone with the loot might never have discovered otherwise. If that were the case, it behooved him to hurry, for once the early afternoon editions appeared with the first reports that stuff would become triply hard to trace.

He paused by the counter and picked up the illustration of the Ritzton coat. "Mind if I take this along, Inspector?"

"Go ahead." The inspector smiled tolerantly. "Gonna chase the loot, Kaw? I wouldn't waste much time on it. As soon as we crack this killing, we'll crack the theft, too." He inclined his head slightly toward the tall man over by the racks, and lowered his voice. "He'll probably loosen up and spill the beans when we get him downtown."

Parry flushed under the collar. To be told that his own efforts were of slight importance was irritating. "Well, I'll see what I can turn up," he murmured, and walked out of the front door.

He had, actually, very little to work on. But a good detective, faced with a scarcity of clues, does not sit on his hands and wait for better ones to develop. He uses what he has.

On Lexington Avenue he stepped into the lobby of the Shelton Hotel and consulted a classified directory. Most of the photographic model agencies were located in the midtown district; he started with the Grand Central Palace Building. In each office he showed the receptionist the picture of the brunette wearing the Ritzton coat, and asked, "That one of your models?" He got ample cooperation, but no results, though in the third place, a petite blonde, after searching the files for half an hour, told him:

"I'm sure her face is familiar. Thornton gets a lot of that garment work; have you tried there?"

HE THANKED her and walked south a few more blocks to the Graybar Building. The foyer of the Thornton offices were lined with full-size photographs of luscious pin-ups, and the redhead behind the desk looked as if she had just stepped out of a magazine cover.

"Why, yes," she said, as soon as he displayed his leaflet. "That's Garda—let me see—Garda— Wait a minute." She stepped to a file and returned with a folder. "Yes. Garda Tudury."

"Do you know where I can find her?" asked Parry.

She regarded him doubtfully. "We're not supposed—"

"It's a legal matter," he said, quickly, smiling.

"She lives on Seventy-Seventh Street. The phone is Trafalgar seven, eight-two-seven-oh."

Parry thanked her, and was in a booth down in the lobby dialing the Trafalgar number almost before he had his hat on.

A feminine voice answered, a high-pitched chirrup. "Yes?"

"Miss Tudury? Miss Garda Tudury?"

"No, I'm her roommate. Who is this?"

"Can you tell me where I can locate her?"

"No, I can't. Who is this calling?"

"Thornton Agency; Stephen Ames, executive vice-president," lied Parry, clearing his throat impressively. "We have a very important assignment for Miss Tudury, and I must reach her right away."

"Oh! The Agency? Oh, I didn't know! Why, she's been working for Noel Aggler, the wholesale firm, on West Thirty-Sixth Street. I think she's going out of town, but you might catch her."

"Thanks very much. I'll try her there."

Parry's face was a little grim as he hurried out and hailed a cab. It looked as if this lead might turn into something after all. The name of Noel Aggler was already so well known to him that he had no need to look up the address. His place was on the ground floor of a loft building in the garment district, where he operated as a wholesaler and middleman in coats, suits, and furs. But he also operated, not quite so openly, as a fence, a shrewd and slippery handler of stolen goods.

Parry's squad had been on his trail more than once, but had never yet quite caught him red-handed. When things got hot, it was Aggler's trick to turn informer, put the finger on the small fry who committed the actual crimes, and thus clear himself. He was not to be trusted as far as you could throw the Brooklyn Bridge.

The taxi snaked through the tangled traffic of the garment district, turned left off Eighth Avenue, and stopped in the middle of the block, double-parked because the curb was lined with trucks. Parry stepped out, handed the driver a five-dollar bill, and waited for change. The driver fumbled through his pockets.

"Here y'are, mister."

But Parry was looking the other way. The display windows of the building in front had been painted dark green on the inside to the height of six or seven feet. Between them a large double door gave easy access to the sidewalk. One half of this door had just opened, and a girl was coming out, smiling back over her shoulder with a little farewell flip of her hand. She was not wearing a Ritzton coat, but Parry recognized her instantly. The trim ankle, the slim figure, the bee-stung lower lip, the big dark eyes—everything matched the photograph in his pocket. She was Grada Tudury.

She closed the door behind her and hurried across the sidewalk to a waiting taxi. In this cab were two large green suitcases, each one close to the dimensions of a steamer trunk, and on the luggage rack next to the driver was an even larger wardrobe trunk. Parry recalled her roommate's words, "I think she's going out of town."

"Hold everything a minute, buddy," he said to his own driver.

The girl climbed into the green cab, leaned forward to speak to her driver. He shifted gears and pulled away from the curb.

Parry jerked the door of his taxi open again. "Put that money back in your pocket. See that green cab, the girl just got in? Stick with it, and the rest of that change is yours."

The driver nodded and let in his clutch.

Behind the show window, unknown to Parry, a sharp-nosed man with big ears and thinning blonde hair had his eye pressed close to the glass where a half-inch slit had been scraped clean, permitting him to peer out without being observed. As Parry's cab shot away, he turned and picked up a telephone, drumming impatiently on the desk until he got his party.

"Sammy? Listen! Garda's just gone off to Grand Central to check those trunks through. There's a young squirt named Kaw, from Safe-and-Loft, tailing her . . . Yeah, that's the one. Better get over there right away and see what he's up to."

PARRY'S cab was close behind at Seventh Avenue and at Sixth. At Fifth Avenue a right-turning truck got in between, and at Madison Avenue he was trapped by a light change. When his driver did manage to wheel north, the green cab was several blocks ahead.

"See if you can make that up," advised Parry.

His driver outflanked a van and scattered pedestrians like pigeons, and was only a block in arrears when their quarry turned right on Forty-Fourth Street. The traffic light blinked red in their faces.

"Go ahead; shoot it!" cried Parry. The driver shot it, grinning.

Wheeling south again on Vanderbilt Avenue, the green cab was nowhere to be seen. However, it was not hard to make a good guess.

"Swing into Grand Central, that

ramp to the baggage room!"

The tires shrieked, and a man growled a curse, as his toes were grazed, but Parry saw the green cab pulling to a stop in front of them. With a curt but grateful, "Good work," to the driver, he jumped out and crossed to the long, brass-surfaced counter.

A red-cap and a baggage clerk in a striped jumper helped the driver unload the three pieces from the green cab and slide them across the counter. The girl rewarded each with a tip and a flashing smile, and drew a ticket from her handbag. Parry stepped close enough to overhear. "The one o'clock train for Boston," but not close enough to make his presence obvious, in the cluster of other travelers that milled about in front of the counter.

The clerk filled out tags and attached them to the trunks, which he then slammed onto a low, flat-bottomed electric truck. They vanished into the cavernous recesses of the baggage room. Parry gazed after them longingly.

How was he to get a look at the contents?

The girl accepted three stubs from the clerk, smiled dazzlingly, and turned away. She crossed the ramp and headed for the stairs that led down to the main concourse. Parry tailed her at a discreet twenty paces.

She crossed the crowded concourse on a diagonal, heedless of the heads that turned to follow her with a second look. Using the revolving door from the Lexington Avenue arcade, she entered the Commodore bar, with Parry close behind. It was too early for the luncheon crowd. She sat down at a table against the wall and picked up a menu. Parry stepped to the bar and asked for a beer.

She had a dry Martini, and then ordered lunch, having more than an hour to wait for her train. But Parry felt time slipping through his fingers. In the arcade he had noticed a stack of fresh newspapers. The afternoon editions were out and he had to act.

He stopped a passing bellhop, pressed a bill into his hand, and said:

"Page Miss Tudury for me—Miss Garda Tudury. I think she's here in the bar. Have her call the B operator."

Then he went to a public booth just outside, dropped in a nickel, and dialed the Commodore. He asked for the B operator, and told her:

"I'm having Miss Tudury paged in the lobby. When she answers, put her on this line, will you, please?"

He waited. When he heard her high heels clacking across the lower foyer, he shut the door of his booth tight. She stepped into a booth opposite, he watched her lift the receiver.

Her voice was rich, husky. "Hello? Who is this?"

Parry made his tone snappily familiar. "Hi, babe? This is Jim, in the office. Listen, Noel wants the numbers of those baggage checks. You've checked the trunks, haven't you?"

She said, "What?" and hesitated. If there was no Jim in the Aggler office, she couldn't be sure of it, and he spoke with the assurance of knowing all about the affair.

"What does he want the numbers for?" she asked.

"In case you lost the stubs, baby. It could happen, you know, and then we'd be in a spot to identify lost baggage."

She mumbled, "Wait a minute." From the tail of his eye Parry could see her digging in her bag. Then he heard her voice again.

"Number twenty-seven, dash, nine-oh-six, nine-oh-seven, and nine-oh-eight."

"Okay, kid. Have a good trip!"

HE SLID the receiver on the hook, and waited until she had re-entered the bar before he left the booth. Then he emerged and cut across to the baggage room at top speed.

The chief baggage clerk was hesitant, even after Parry showed his badge and talked about stolen merchandise.

"Stolen? I don't know nothin' about that. Right now they're the responsibility of the railroad, and I have to get authority from—"

"Well, you start getting it," urged Parry. "Meanwhile I'll take one of your handlers and locate the pieces, and by the time you get the okay we'll be all set."

Without saying so in so many words, Parry conveyed the impression that he would do nothing further until official permission had been received. The chief clerk nodded, and reached for his phone.

The handler said, "The one o'clock for Boston? That'll be down at the east end. Come through this way."

The vast room was a maze of aisles between mountains and molehills of luggage. White lines painted on the floor marked off areas, and hanging signs carried numbers and cabalistic symbols. Numerous elevator shafts led to the train platforms below. Hand trucks, electric trucks, and laden porters moved busily about.

Parry's guide led him through the bedlam expertly, and paused before one of the smaller stacks.

"Here we are. What are those stub numbers now?"

Parry spotted the wardrobe trunk immediately. He checked the number, then dragged it out in the open and set it up on end. Hunkering on his heels in front of it, he reached in his pocket.

It was his business, on the Safe-and-Loft Squad, to get in and out of locked doors, and he carried a collection of skeleton keys that any burglar would have been tickled to death to own. For that reason Parry carried them chained to his waist-band. It was the third key, plus a little expert pressure in the right direction, that did the trick. The wardrobe trunk swung open.

Parry could not repress a little grunt of triumph. His eyes narrowed, and he sniffed eagerly. What was it the doctor had called it? *Cuir de Russie*—Russian leather. It was an unusual perfume, certainly and he could not remember ever having smelled it before today. Still, it was not wholly unique. The owner of the Shir-Lee Shoppe could not have been the *only* woman in New York to use it. What he had so far was a good clue, but it was not definite proof.

He lifted out one of the Ritzton coats, held it up to the light, and examined it closely. He buried his nose in the fur collar, and nodded. But when he lifted out a second coat and sniffed at the collar, he got the same odor, though less strongly. He realized that, packed tightly together like this, the aroma had been transmitted from one garment to the next. The exact coat worn by Shirley Leeton, alias Roszinda Skoviescher, was still anonymous, unprovable.

He pulled out three or four more, peered at them keenly. Then quickly he repacked them, marking the last one he had examined by turning up a couple inches of one cuff. He was just closing the trunk when the baggage master strode up.

"They say—hey, have you been inside that trunk?"

"Just a peek," said Parry, "to be sure it's the one I want. You got permission all right, didn't you?"

The man nodded. "To take them to Police Headquarters, not to open them up here. But you'll have to give me a receipt."

"Okay, I'll give you a receipt." Parry helped the handler load the three pieces on a hand truck, and told him, "Run them out to the ramp and load them in a taxi for me, will you? Tell the driver to wait. I'll be right out."

Parry followed the chief clerk into his office. Here the clerk inserted carbon paper into a pad of printed forms, and began to fill in the blanks with dates, names, stub numbers and descriptions. He wrote with exasperating slowness.

"Can I use your phone?" asked Parry, picking up the instrument as he spoke. He got Police Headquarters, then after a moment's delay reached Inspector Draper.

"Parry Kaw, Inspector. I've got the loot from the Shir-Lee Shoppe. Being checked through Grand Central in some trunks."

"The devil you have!" cried the inspector. "Are you sure?"

"Absolutely, and there's a positive tie-in that will stand up in court," Parry told him. "It's passed through the hands of a fence; Noel Aggler, on West Thirty-Sixth Street. You might send one of the boys over to pick him up."

"You mean Aggler killed that woman?"

PARRY KAW smiled and slowly shook his head. When he spoke, his tone was incisive.

"No. He probably wasn't even there. But he'll welch on the source of his merchandise as fast as he finds there was a murder involved, don't worry. And after he does that, we've got him as a receiver of stolen property. And there's a model sitting in the Commodore bar who you'd better pick up, too. She's eating chicken a la king, has a Martini glass with an olive pit in it in front of her, and is by all odds the most beautiful girl in the place. Furthermore, her picture is on that Ritzton coat circular. She may be only a stooge, to get the stuff out of the city—I hope! But you'll need her as a witness, to link the trunks to Noel Aggler. . . Yes, I'm bringing them down right away. See you in a few minutes, Inspector."

He scrawled his name and shield number on the bottom of the receipt pad, folded a carbon copy and tucked it in his pocket, and emerged from the office very well satisfied with himself. But he was counting his chickens before they were hatched.

The handler was nowhere in sight. A taxicab was just pulling away on the ramp. A wardrobe trunk was lashed next to the driver, and two large suitcases were stowed inside. There were also two men inside, complete strangers to Parry, one of whom was leaning forward to speak instructions into the driver's ear.

Parry cried, "Hey!" and vaulted the counter. But the cab was already swinging the turn at the end of the ramp.

The next taxi in line had just discharged a couple of elderly women, who were both fumbling in their handbags. Parry leaped in front next to the driver.

"Follow that cab that just pulled out!" he shouted, and flashed his shield. "Never mind their fare—I'll pay it!" He saw the driver pale, but the cab shot ahead. "And step on it!"

As they careened the bend at the lower end of the ramp, he saw the cab ahead making a right turn into Forty-Sixth Street. "There he goes! Get up behind him now!"

As they wheeled into the cross street the light at Lexington Avenue was red, but it changed to green before they had completed the turn. They picked up yardage, because the cab ahead had come to a stop, and had to start up again. But at the corner they were blocked.

East Lexington Avenue, Forty-Sixth is a one-way street, but both curbs were lined with parked cars, narrowing it to two lanes. A huge van attempted a right turn from the avenue, found too little room to swing, and had to back and fill. They waited, Parry cursing, and watching the other cab, which had slipped by reach Third Avenue and turn south.

When at last they squeezed past the van themselves, Parry barked, "Pay no attention to lights! Go after them!"

The driver muttered, "What is it, copper? A hold-up?"

"No, just a store burglar," replied Parry quickly. "I don't expect they're carrying any guns."

"I got a wife and kids," muttered the driver, but he pressed the accelerator to the floor.

They gained ground on Third Avenue, lost it on a turn to the east, and then made up most of it racing down First Avenue, lacing in and out of moving columns of trucks. They were half a block behind, a mile from their starting point, when the cab ahead made a sudden left turn to the east.

This cross street, obstacled by parked vehicles loading and unloading, led to the foot of an open pier, where it ended. The cab did not slow, but drove straight out on the pier. Some barges and scows were tied up on one side, a rusty tramp steamer on the other. The cab went on past them, all the way to the end, where it made a quarter circle and stopped close to the stringpiece. The doors opened and both passengers piled out.

"Pull up behind them—quick!" Parry told his driver.

He guessed their intentions right away. Those two strangers, involved in the crime, had discovered that a murder charge was in the offing. The value of the stolen coats was nothing compared to the risk of the hot seat. So to wipe their trail clean, they were going to ditch any and all evidence at the bottom of the East River.

ALREADY they had their hands on the wardrobe trunk. Parry sprang to the ground, yelling. Their heads turned in alarm. He saw that one man was slim and short, with a bony nose and narrow, treacherous eyes. The other man was a huge hulk of a bruiser with the facial expression of a bull and hands like hams.

Parry's driver, failing to brake completely, rammed into the rear end of the parked cab with a rude jolt. If intentional, it was a happy inspiration. The jerk threw both the crooks off balance, the trunk slipped on the running board, and the big man fell. Perry promptly went after the other one.

His features contorted into a sneer, the little man reached under his coat lapel for a weapon. Parry hit him before he could grasp it. The small thug recoiled, staggering. He was in a dilemma—either he had to put up his hands to defend himself or use them to go after his gun. He never had time to make a decision. Parry's second blow, to the pit of the stomach, doubled him up. The third, a short upper-cut put out the lights.

At a yell from his driver, Parry's head jerked around. The big man, having regained his feet, was charging like a tank at full speed. Parry took one look at two hundred and fifty pounds of angry bone and muscle, and like a flash dropped to hands and knees.

The big man could not check his rush. With a loud cry, he pitched headforemost over Parry's crouching form. One heavy shot smacked Parry's side, cracking a rib and driving the wind from his lungs. The sound of a strong splash came up from the surface of the river, ten feet below the stringpiece, and on the next pier some men began shouting and waving their arms.

A couple of hours later Parry sat in the small room next to Inspector Draper's office, down at Headquarters. His chest had been bandaged and taped, but it hurt, and would continue to hurt for many weeks, every time he drew a deep breath. Through the closed door he could hear the steady murmur of voices as the questioning went on and on. He smiled contentedly. The door opened. Inspector Draper, his eyes angry, came through, closing it behind him.

"Look here, Kaw, these birds are holding out on us." he said disgustedly. "They're trying to claim we've got hold of a different bunch of coats entirely. Now you told me that you had a positive tie-in. What was it?"

Parry smiled gently. "Did you open the trunk yet?"

"Certainly we opened it. It's full of Ritzton coats that are just like any other Ritzton coats. Of course that perfume is on them—what do you call it? Russian stuff. But that's not enough. There might be a thousand women who used that perfume. It won't pin that coat to Shirley what's-her-name, in court."

"Did you notice that the sleeve on one of those coats is turned back a couple of inches?"

"Come to think of it, yes. What of it?"

"If you will take that coat into a good strong light, and examine the fur collar, you will see that there are a couple of hairs clinging to the fur, right at the back of the neck. Human hairs, dark and short, about the length that would come out of a feather-cut. Those hairs can be put under a microscope, and by comparison with other hairs can be identified positively as belonging to a certain head. Unless I'm wrong, your laboratory experts—"

"By golly, Kaw, you've got something there!" exclaimed the inspector, his eyes beginning to shine. He turned toward the door, then turned back again. "You know, for a trick like that, we ought to be able to get you transferred to Homicide!"

Parry held up his hand. "No, thanks. He grinned, knowing that the inspector had just paid him his highest compliment. "I'm very happy, on Safe-and-Loft, thanks just the same." Then, in view of the occasion, he permitted himself a slight gesture of swagger.

"But any time you need help with a murder case, Inspector," he added with a generous sweep of his hand, "I'll be glad to lend a hand, of course."

•

"Come on out, Lieutenant," Stan called, and the dark man stepped out of the closet

Death Is the ANSWER

By JOHN D. MacDONALD

Professor Quotient's quiz act suddenly pays off in grim murder, with a baffling mystery as the jackpot question!

LEANING back in the wicker hotel chair, Thomas Gaylord Schurtz gobbled a good half of a Tom Collins. He was in his pajamas and robe. He slapped his protruding paunch and said, "Ah! The world brightens!" He was a big red-faced man, with iron gray hair and big red hands. Ex-carnival barker. Ex-picker of coal. Ex-stevedore. A man with a voice like burnished brass and a laugh that was contagious.

At the moment he was Professor

Quotient. It was not hard work, standing on the stage of a theater while slim Mary Adams, in sequined tights and bra, stood by holding the bowl of folded questions, the program notes. Two bright kids, Nick Wellar and Stan Haverly, plus a few local boys picked up for a five each, roamed through the audience with the hand mikes and trailing cords, singling out extroverts in the audience to answer the questions and get paid off in crisp dollar bills—or crisp fifties for the jackpot question of the evening. It was a national hookup, selling the bleating public a mouth wash made of alcohol, water, and peppermint flavoring. A thousand a week. Four hundred for Nick, Stan, and Mary for salaries and expenses. Five hundred clear for Thomas Gaylord Schurtz, alias Professor Quotient. A big deal. A fine fat deal.

Sometimes Tom Schurtz wondered how long it would last. That thought always made him vaguely uncomfortable. He wasn't saving a dime. Not a dime. But, heck, when folks got tired of this, something else would pop up. It had to. It always had so far.

Mary Adams sat by the window reading *Variety*. She was trim and dark, with wide eyes and that peculiar little touch of calm self-possession which comes to any girl who must stand before large audiences with no defense but her smile and her figure. Mary kept the job because it paid well. Without its ever being said aloud, Nick, Tom and Stan knew that she was the balance wheel, the foil, the symbol of unity. With a word and a glance she could salve Nick's self-esteem, quiet Tom's temper, ease Stan's basic loneliness. With another type of glance she could freeze a pass by an eager male before it got well started.

Nick Wellar was spread out on a bed, wearing a soft yellow sport shirt and dark green gabardine trousers. He was swinging one leg and humming at the ceiling. He was tall and straight, with the kind of good looks that are admired in Naples, Lisbon and Madrid. He moved like a bull fighter and talked with all the good humor and intelligence of a ten-cent slot machine.

Nick Wellar had three standard daydreams. The first was that he would take over Tom's job. The second was that he would punch the ears off of Stan Haverly. The third was that Mary would accelerate her slow process of falling in love with him.

STAN HAVERLY was the outsider, a slow, careful lad who would have been considered handsome in Sweden, Bavaria or Princeton. In fact he had been to Princeton where he had taken work in mass psychology and the psychology of advertising. To him, his job was a clinic. He kept detailed notes on audience reaction and an analysis of humor. Stan Haverly knew that it might take ten years or twenty years, but eventually he would be known in a hundred plush offices in Manhattan as the man to see regarding program construction and audience reaction. He was careful, self-contained, scorned a bit by Tom and Nick as an outsider who was in, but not of, the entertainment world.

Tom Schurtz had hired Nick and Stan because they were clean-cut, they had voices that fit the airwaves and they knew instinctively how to handle the public. He was satisfied with both of them, and especially with Nick. Tom had picked Mary with the knowledge gained from looking at ten thousand women. He knew that each audience was filled with young men to whom the questions were just a roar of sound in their ears and who walked out of the theater in a state of numb entrancement. She could do more by just standing and holding the bowl of questions than most women could do in a lead spot with Martha Graham.

Tom gulped the rest of his drink and said, "Ah! Soon, my children, we must prepare to face our public in this thriving metropolis of Hoagersburg."

Mary glanced up from *Variety*. "Thriving metropolis on the outer fringes of civilization, Thomas. Phone for the dog team."

"Break it off, my dear," Tom said. "We always fill their largest theater, don't we? An audience in West Overshoe, New Hampshire, is no different than a small group packing the Yankee Stadium. As I have so often said—people are folks."

"You used to say, 'Skin the marks. They're asking for it.' Are you mellowing?" Nick asked.

Stan put on his professorial manner. "Marks—an ancient carnival word used to denote the cash customers. Now they are more generally called 'yaks'."

"Okay, Doctor Haverly," Nick said. "Speaking of yaks, how about our usual bet? Our two-man pool? Are you on for a five?"

Mary grinned at Tom and said, "So again we have the five-dollar contest between practise and theory. With practise winning again."

"Theory is right," Stan moaned. "I don't get it. My records say that out of the last seven times, you've won six. Six times you've handed out more dough on right answers than I have. What do you do? Whisper the answers? Or do you split with Tom?"

"Leave me out of this," Tom said. "I make it a point to give you and Nick the same number of questions, equally difficult. And they add up to about the same amount of payoff. You guys both know what's in the bowl. Nick just has a better eye for—for—"

"The extroverted intelligentsia," Mary supplied.

"Yeah. You bother me, Mary. You're beginning to sound like Doctor Haverly here. Anyway, since you so kindly supplied the words to fit my thought, I will rephrase. Nick has an eye for smarter people. How are you guys lined up for tonight?"

"I'm right balcony and Stan's front and center," Nick said, "You didn't tell me, Stan boy. Is it a bet?"

"You're twenty-five ahead. I must bet to protect my investment."

"Run along, children," Tom said, getting to his feet with a grunt. "Time to get ready."

Mary and Stan, as usual, had single rooms down the hall from the double occupied by Tom and Nick. They left the room together, and Stan saw a look on Nick's face that told him that Nick didn't like the idea of their going anywhere together.

Stan told himself that Nick had no cause for alarm. It was true that he couldn't look into Mary's eyes without a small feeling of shock, but something always made him blundering and stupid when he was with her. He knew it was the gulf between them caused by the job. To Mary, the job was a part of her career. To Stan the job was a training ground, a source of data, an amusing and relatively unimportant phase. He could understand her attitude, but he doubted whether she could understand him. So he made no effort to see if she could understand. With an odd feeling of loss, he watched her gravitate toward Nick.

Suddenly she caught his arm. He looked at her in surprise.

"Hold up there, Professor. You just walked by your room."

Stan blushed and turned back, looking over his shoulder to admire the way she walked down the hall. He stood for a time in his room, staring out of his window at a blank brick wall, his forehead knotted, trying to figure out why he was so easily beaten by Nick each week. . . .

THE Ajax Theater was loaded. Eager citizens who couldn't find seats were herded behind the aged velvet ropes held by the pimply ushers.

The curtain went up and Tom walked out, shining in white tie and tails. He grinned at the audience, patted the top of the mike and said, "I'm Professor Quotient and friend. Neither of us kill ourselves working." As usual he got a good laugh. "You've all heard this program over the radio. But on the radio, you can't see Mary. Come out here, Mary." She came out in her sequined tights and bra, holding the bowl of questions. Tom killed the stomping and whistling by holding up both hands. "This is called a warm up. I'm supposed to make you happy, so when we go on the air Mary and I get what's called 'thunderous applause'."

As usual, they ate it up. Tom glanced out into the wings and then at his watch. "We have time for a little instruction—not that all you bright people need it. I know you're all here loaded with facts and figures. I'll pull a question out of the bowl and my assistants in the audience will pick out somebody to answer it. When they hand you that mike, don't be afraid of it. Talk up. Make

Aunt Minnie in Tuxedo Junction understand every word. I'll announce the value of the question before I ask it. Okay, folks, here comes my announcer. We're about ready for the air. Get ready now. Make with the hands when I tell you. Okay. Now! *Hit it!*"

The announcer said, "And now, from the stage of the Ajax Theater in Hoagersburg we present the one—the only—Professor Quotient—one half hour of fun and games brought to you by the manufacturers of Amoeba Mouthwash, the blue bottle that knocks off those germs . . . ."

Stan Haverly, in the aisle, front and center, examined the faces of the customers. That kid on the aisle, smirking, greased hair. Stay away from him. Wise. And don't pick anybody near that drunk. He might get cute and try to say something into the mike. Cute young girl there that might do. Pick 'em bright tonight. Get back one of those fives from Nick. Take the cute gal for the first one. He strolled nearer to her, and she gave him a half-frightened, sideways look. He bent over her and said, "Want to try one?"

She compressed her lips and nodded.

The commercial was through. Tom was on again, saying, "And remember that the last question, folks, is the jackpot question. All money not won during the rest of the program gets loaded on the jackpot question. Mary here will write the growing amount of the jackpot on this blackboard. Keep watching it. Tonight we're starting it off with a hundred dollars. Watch it grow. Now for the first question. Stan?"

Stan depressed the switch on his hand mike. "A young lady here would like to try one, sir. Your name and address, Miss. Please speak directly into the microphone."

A shy monotone. "Winifred Higby. Eleven Tyler Crescent."

"Now, Winifred," Tom said, "your question will pay you five crisp one-dollar bills if you answer it correctly. It's a music question. What well known jazz musician, a guitarist, recently opened a restaurant in New York? He is famous for his unique use of the English language. Come, now. Ten seconds."

The girl flushed and chewed her lip, looking up at Stanley hopelessly.

"Quickly, now," Tom said. "No prompting by you people seated near her. Don't know? Winifred, it's the one, the only, Eddie Condon. Give the girl a ticket, Stanley, entitling her to one bottle of that great Amoeba Mouthwash. Mary, add that five dollars to the jackpot. The jackpot is now worth one hundred and five dollars. Nick? Do you have someone?"

The half hour scurried by. Stan knew that his luck was out. Only two of the people he selected were able to answer correctly. Nick's selections missed, too, but not so often. The prizes grew larger. Ten dollars. Twenty dollars. Fifty dollars. The audience was eager and excited. The two stand-ins in other parts of the theater didn't have as much luck as Nick.

Stan glanced at his watch. The questions were over. Only the jackpot question was left. By mutual agreement, Nick and he left the jackpot question off the pool. There was too much money involved. Stan knew that he was silly to be so concerned about the five-dollar pool that it took his mind off his real work, that of gauging and analyzing the audience reactions to standard situations. He would have notes to write up when he got back to his room.

It didn't bother him that Nick was Tom's obvious favorite, was given the assignments to check theaters, to make lighting arrangements, to hire the additional men needed to cover the audiences, to make a lot of the travel arrangements. It was work that Stan wasn't interested in. What did bother him was the way that Nick could consistently win their childish pool. Was it as Mary had hinted, that Nick had a better eye for people, a better ability to gauge intelligence by outward appearance? Possibly. But it wouldn't do any good to dwell on that thought.

As ALWAYS, Stan's mind began to wander off the subject at hand. He didn't have to pay much attention, Nick was always given the jackpot question assignment. By habit, he always devoted the last few minutes of the program to thoughts of Mary. She was easy to think about, and easy to see, standing up there, straight and slim, her smile deep and friendly. If only— But what was the use? She was show people. There would always be a gulf between them. But it was becoming increasingly difficult to travel with Nick, Tom and Mary, and watch Mary slowly fall in love with Nick. He wasn't good enough to her.

Stan fought his way out of these depressing thoughts in time to hear Tom say, "Thank you, Nick, for finding us a brave man willing to tackle the jackpot question. Now hold that bale of money up where Mr. Bostwick, our candidate, can see it, Nick. Like the looks of that, Mr. Bostwick? It's all yours if you can answer one little question I'm going to ask you. Four hundred and twenty dollars for thirty little seconds of effort. Ready? It's a question on mathematics. Mental arithmetic. And it's a toughy. Here is the question. Using four nines —the figure nine—can you arrange them in such a way that they will equal one hundred? Do anything you want with them, but use them all, and don't use any other figures along with them. Thirty seconds, Mr. Bostwick. Go!"

The audience was hushed. They were all trying to work the problem. Mr. Bostwick mumbled into the mike, "Now if you took ninety-nine point nine nine that would be almost—"

"Almost isn't good enough, Mr. Bostwick. Your time is running short. You're warm though. Think hard now."

"Lemme see now," Mr. Bostwick mused. "Hey! What about ninety-nine and nine ninths?"

"What about it?" Tom roared. "Man, you got it! You got it! Nick, give Mr. Bostwick the four hundred and twenty dollars. Nice work, Mr. Bostwick." He had to wait for the applause to die away. "And now folks, since that is all we have time for, I'll turn you over to the announcer who wants to tell you something about our sponsor's product and our plans for next week. Thank you all."

STAN awoke with the telephone screaming at him. He felt as though he had been asleep a long time. He clicked on the reading lamp and groped for the phone, squinting.

"Yeah?" he mumbled into the receiver.

It was Tom. "Stan, boy. Climb into your clothes. Nick has had trouble. I'm dressing. Meet you down in the lobby." Click.

So Nick was in trouble. Nothing unusual, but this time it must be something pretty serious. Stan dashed the sleep out of his face with cold water and dressed hurriedly. Tom, jittery and impatient, had a taxi waiting.

On the way to the hospital he gave Stan the bare outlines. Nick had been picked up in an alley earlier in the evening in bad shape. Slugged. His wallet was gone and it had taken quite a while to figure out who he was. Fortunately one of the nurses remembered seeing him at the theater. The police were with him, hoping he would come out of it long enough to talk. Tom had given orders to have him moved from the ward to a private room.

The brisk interne wasted no words. "Gentlemen, he's in bad shape. Depressed fracture. Struck with some kind of blunt weapon over the right ear. We operated immediately, hoping to remove the pressure. We have, but there is a sliver of bone driven down into the brain. If we can pull him out of his severe postoperative shock, we'll be able to get that bone sliver. Otherwise—" The interne shrugged and made a flat chopping motion with the edge of his hand. Tom winced.

The lean, dark man beside the bed introduced himself in a hushed voice. "I'm Lieutenant Bandred. Sorry this had to happen here. I'm waiting to see if he can give us a hint as to who slugged him. I've got men out trying to trace his movements, but it's hard with all the joints closed now. He was in the worst section of town."

Nick's swarthy face was gray against the pillow. There were deep lines around the corners of his mouth. His head was lightly bandaged and a nurse stood by to help in case he regained consciousness and started to roll over to the right. Tom stood at the foot of the bed and made fumbling motions with his big red hands.

"He'll be okay. He's a good kid. He'll

be okay," he muttered.

Nick's mouth twitched. There was no sound in the room. Tom and Stan moved closer to Nick. The nurse bent over him. The lieutenant hitched his chair a bit closer. Nick's eyes and mouth opened slowly. The eyes were wet and glazed. The lips looked dry. The nurse made a hissing noise and the interne hurried in.

Nick's damp eyes seemed to focus on Tom. His underlip flapped. "Belt," he said clearly. "Margi—"

Then his body strained upward, sweat beading his face. The nurse touched his forehead. There was a guttural, dry sound in his throat, and the eyes closed again. The swarthy face seemed to shrink into the pillow, to diminish. Stan had seen it happen before, on the beaches of jungle islands. He turned away. The interne stepped forward with a stethoscope. When Stan turned around again, the face was hidden by the top of the sheet. Tom gulped and stood stricken for a moment. Stan saw the reassurance flood back into him.

"That's too bad," Tom said. "He was a good boy. I'll miss him. I'll contact his folks. Stan, you get hold of a local undertaker."

Lieutenant Bandred stood up, wearily. He looked like a man who had had a long, difficult night. "Guess it's not necessary to tell you folks how much I'm sorry that this thing had to happen in Hoagersburg. We'll sure do our best on it. How long will you folks stay around?"

"We were leaving tomorrow. Let's see. Today is Thursday. We can stay until Monday."

"I sure hope we'll be able to nail the guy that did this thing before then. I've got every exit from town blocked, and we're pulling in every bum that tries to slip out. What do you think he meant by that belt stuff, and Margy?"

Tom sighed. "Don't know. Guess he was saying he got belted on the head. And Margy was probably some gal friend. I don't think you'll get much of a lead. Stan, boy, do me a favor. You stay here and go through his stuff. I'll do the same back at the hotel. I'll have to tell Mary and wire New York for a replacement. I guess he can be shipped back to his folks in Chicago in what he was wearing, if they aren't messed up."

"His clothes weren't soiled. The wound didn't bleed," the nurse said.

Tom left. Nick's clothes were still down in the emergency room. It was a nasty job going through the pockets. Cigarettes. Gold lighter. Money clip with twenty bucks in it. Stan held the money and frowned. He stuffed it into his own pocket. Handkerchief. Nick had said something about a belt. Could be a belt on the head. Could be the belt he was wearing. Ordinary looking belt. Imitation alligator with a gold-plated buckle. Stan rubbed his fingers along it. It seemed rather thick. On a hunch he stripped it out of the loops on the trousers. His fingers began to tremble when he noticed a zipper on the underside of it. A trick belt. Obviously the lieutenant had missed it and Tom hadn't known about it.

Stan glanced around. No one was watching him. He slid the zipper back, disclosing two flat packs of bills folded the long way. Hundreds. A couple of five hundreds. He picked the bills out of the belt and crammed them into his pocket. He rethreaded the belt through the trouser loops. Odd that Nick should have so much money. Several thousand by the feel of it. And apparently Nick wanted the money sent to somebody named Margy. Margy who? And where? An odd setup.

IT WAS gray dawn when the taxi pulled up in front of the hotel. A man in the hotel uniform pulled himself out of a lobby chair and yawned as he took Stan up in the elevator. The transom over Tom's door showed an oblong of yellow light. Stan knocked lightly, turned the knob and walked in. Tom was still dressed, slumped in the wicker chair. His red face looked tired and drawn, his gray hair rumpled. Mary, in a maroon robe, sat on the edge of a bed, her face puffed and streaked with tears. She was through crying. Her eyes were calm, and dead.

"Sit down, Stan. Sit down. Have a drink," Tom said.

There was a bottle of rye and a glass on a table by the window. Stan walked over, poured out an inch of rye and threw it down. It bit his throat and nearly gagged him. He sat on the bed several feet away from Mary.

"This sort of breaks things up, my boy," Tom said.

"How so? You're going on with the show, aren't you?"

"Oh, yes. We'll go on. But losing Nick has made me realize what an empty life I'm leading. I looked on that boy as a son. I'm getting old, Stanley, and I get lonelier every day. I need someone. I've been talking to Mary. She has consented to be my wife."

Stan held his face rigid and then forced a slow smile. He looked at Mary. She was staring at the floor, the smoke from her cigarette winding up in a pale gray thread, as gray as the dawn outside.

"You have my congratulations, Tom. You know that. I hope you'll both be happy. Let's talk about Nick in the morning. I'll see you then." He felt shocked and unbelieving, but he couldn't let them see it. Either of them. He managed to walk to the door, say good-night to them and shut it softly behind him. When he got back to his own room he sat on the edge of his rumpled bed. To take his mind away from Mary, he took Nick's money out and counted it. Six thousand, six hundred dollars. Too much. Something wrong somewhere. But where?

He lifted his head as he heard Mary's soft footsteps in the hall. He heard her door close. He got up and went down to her door and knocked. She opened it, saw him, and said, "What is it, Stan?"

"Could I come in for just a minute, Mary? I want to talk to you."

She held the door open and he walked in. The room was identical with his own. She sat near the window and he sat on the edge of the bed. She looked defeated, completely and utterly tired.

"Why are you doing it, Mary?" he asked, gently.

Her head snapped up, and her eyes widened. "Aren't you a little out of your area, junior? I'm marrying him because he needs me. Because this thing has nearly licked him. You, bright eyes, don't know what it means to a woman to be needed."

[*Turn page*]

"Suppose I told you that I needed you, too?"

"Hah! A lovely thought. You and Nick. Both self-sufficient. You, because you've got the brains. Nick, because he knew all the angles. You two needed me like I need holes in the head."

"You'd like to think you're hard and tough, wouldn't you, Mary?" he asked.

Her face crumpled a little. "Not me, Stan. There's no toughness in me."

"Why are you doing it?" he asked again.

Their eyes met. Hers, bright with anger, shifted and changed, as he watched. He suddenly knew that he loved her, that it was a desperate, aching love that had been growing under the surface for months. He looked at her and knew that she saw it in his eyes.

Her voice was almost a sob. "Stan, why did you have to wait until now? Until too late. Couldn't you see? Couldn't you tell long before this?"

"Go back now and tell him that you won't marry him."

She stiffened. "Get out of here. I gave my word. He's my sort and you're not. Get out."

Back in his own room he pulled a chair around until it faced the window. The sky was growing lighter. He smoked cigarettes until there was a staleness in his mouth. He sensed that there were factors in his mind that could be added, if he knew how. A master quiz with a giant jackpot. Things that seemed disconnected, disassociated. Tom standing up there on the platform, dipping his left hand into the bowl held by Mary. Nick out in the audience, giving the customers a look at the money they might win. Nick winning the five-dollar pools. Nick making the arrangements. Nick and Tom and Mary sorting out the questions for the next week's program. Trick questions. Quick questions.

He sensed that there were conclusions that could be drawn, if he could only sort out the pertinent factors.

And who was Margy?

AT LAST he laid across the bed, fully clothed, and caught an hour of restless sleep. When he awakened, his clothes were sodden with chill perspiration and his mouth tasted sour and dry. He sat on the edge of the bed, remembering how Mary's eyes had said something entirely different from the sharp words that had come from her lips. Their relationship was like an intricate problem in a game of chess. Each piece balanced another, and then an unexpected move had eliminated Nick. The regrouping of pieces, the different pressures of forces and circumstances, had placed the pawn labeled "Mary" under the influence of the major piece labeled "Tom Schurtz."

He took a long shower, and as he was shaving, the last words that Nick had spoken kept running through his mind. The belt had been explained. Not Margy. Stan began to repeat softly all the words he could think of that started with Margy: Marjorie, margarine, marjoram, Margin— Margin? What sort of margin? On what? He stopped shaving, his razor in midair, staring into the eyes of the troubled stranger in the mirror. Margin! It could be! It might be! It *had* to be!

He finished hurriedly and dressed, fumbling with the buttons in his excitement. As soon as the waiter arrived with the orange juice and coffee, Stan made his phone call. It took quite a few minutes to convince Lieutenant Bandred that he wasn't delirious. And another five minutes to get Bandred's cooperation.

By ten o'clock the arrangements were completed. Stan knocked on Tom's door and walked in. Tom was sitting on the edge of his bed, in lurid pajamas, yawning and stretching his gray head. His cheeks looked sunken and mottled.

"I woke up, Stan," Tom said, "and I couldn't figure out why I felt so bad until I remembered Nick. It all seems like a bad dream, doesn't it?"

"It sure does," Stan agreed soberly. "Look, Tom. Get your robe on and come down to my room. I've got something I want to show you."

"Sure, lad. But can't you bring it up here?"

"I'd rather do it this way. I'll tell you when you get there."

"Okay, if you insist. A mystery, hey? I'll be along in a couple of minutes."

[*Turn page*]

Stan was sitting on the bed when Tom came in, yawning, and shut the door behind him. The single armchair by the window faced the bed. Tom walked heavily over to it and sat down. He yawned again.

"Give it to me, Stanley boy," he said then. "What's the mystery?"

Stan lowered his voice and said, "I think I better get a little more dough. Say twice as much as I'm getting now. That's for a starter."

Tom lifted his lips in a painted smile, exposing his wet teeth. His eyes didn't smile. "What makes you so valuable, son?"

"I know how Nick fixed the pool now, Tom."

"Fixed the pool! You got a fever?"

"No. Let me give you the angle. Nick went ahead and checked the theaters, didn't he? So what did he do each time? He went to a bar and selected a few smart looking guys. He took these citizens aside and showed them how to make a few bucks. He told them to get to the theater early and sit in the exact seats he selected for them. Then he selected those guys for the questions with the big payoff and gave them the answers so they could collect. But he never paid them the entire amount. He would bend over and count out about half the amount and pocket the rest."

"You're yammering like crazy, Stanley. How the heck could he tell them the answers?" Tom objected.

"Too easy. We do the act with the house lights on. The seats he picked for the wise guys are right under the ceiling lights. We all know the answers to the questions and we all know that as the program goes along, the payoff gets higher. Before the show Nick picked eight or ten short answers to the questions we're going to use, and printed them on the margins of the crisp new bills, using a very soft pencil. He could always turn a printed answer into a smudge with his thumb. He had already told the guys he contacted to look at the margin of the bill he held in front of them for the answer. All he had to do was keep the bills straight in his hand, the ones with the answers."

"That's fantastic!" Tom exploded.

"You think so?" Stan asked with a thin smile. "Somebody always manages to knock off that jackpot question—nearly always. People aren't that bright. Also, Nick always got more winners than I did. That's against the law of percentages. And, to cap it off, Nick told me."

"Told you!" Tom stared at him coldly.

"Certainly. You already knew how he was doing it. Maybe it was your idea. But you didn't catch on when he mumbled something about Margy. He was trying to say margin."

"What has that got to do with me, son? Suppose he was working an angle? Why should you claim that I knew about it?"

"Go ahead," Stan said and shrugged. "Be tough, Tom. If I can't convince you, maybe the cops can. You know, they might say that an old hand like you could sense whether or not a question was likely to be answered correctly."

TOM folded his red hands over his stomach. He said, "Stanley, when you mention the police you put this little talk on a different plane. Continue, please."

"Okay. You and Nick were in this together. You shouldn't have trusted Nick. That was a mistake. You were splitting half the jackpot on each program plus half of the fee for five or six other questions. Nick realized that he could blow you sky high if he talked. You had a lot more to lose than he did. A few little words and you'd be out of radio. Then how would you make a living? Being smart, Nick started to taper off your end of the take. At last he was taking it all, and then he put the bite on you for a little in addition."

"Keep talking." Tom's face was grim.

"Glad to," Stan said obligingly. "You're quite a guy, Tom. How about you and Mary? I'll bet you've been wanting her for a long time and you had to sit around and watch her falling in love with Nick. That hurt, didn't it? Then you saw the combination. Knock Nick off and catch Mary on the bounce. Good applied psychology. Also it took the pressure off you. What did Nick say before you slugged him in that alley?"

[Turn page]

"You haven't got enough, Stanley."

"Not even with the sixty-six hundred bucks I found in Nick's belt?" Stan taunted him. "You were anxious to be the one to go through his luggage. I took a look at it. That wasn't bright, Tom, slicing the linings when you were looking for Nick's money. And how about the act? How many people have seen you dip into that bowl with your left hand? Remember, Tom, Nick was slugged over the right ear."

"Where's the dough?" Tom demanded in a tight voice.

"Oh, the money? Over in the top drawer of the bureau. I feel sorry for you, Tom. You missed in too many ways. You never should have let Nick make those greedy little five-dollar bets with me. That's what started me thinking that he worked it in a crooked manner."

Tom smiled again, and his big lips pressed back thin and tight against his teeth. "This has been mighty white of you, Stanley. Let me tell you that I love you like my own son. I hate to do this to you, but I just can't see jumping from the pan to the fire, like the fellow says. It's tough on my nerves. And sixty-six hundred bucks is good nerve cure. See this thing? It's a thirty-two automatic. I better tell the folks that you put up a battle trying to hold onto a thousand bucks that you found in Nick's luggage. I can mark myself up a little with my own fist, I guess. And maybe I better tell them that you weren't in your room last night, that I met you in the lobby as I was heading for the hospital. You won't be able to contradict, son."

"How long do you think it'll be before one of Nick's suckers in one of the towns we've played starts to talk?" Stan demanded.

Tom inspected the small gun and swung the muzzle toward Stan. "Never in this here world thought I'd end up killing both you boys," he said with a harsh giggle.

Stan's mouth went suddenly dry. "There's a thirty-eight aimed right at your head, Tom," he said. "Lieutenant Bandred is in the closet with the door opened just far enough. Come on out, Lieutenant."

The lean dark man stepped out of the closet and took the small automatic out of Thomas Gaylord Schurtz's limp hand. "Sure glad we were able to clean this up before you got out of town, Mr. Schurtz. All this makes me feel better about it happening here, though." He turned to Stan and said, "You cut it pretty close, Haverly."

"I had to. He didn't admit it until the last. And there wasn't any real proof."

Tom sat collapsed in the chair, staring at the far wall. The brass had gone out of his voice as he said, "Right on almost everything. Except I didn't want to kill Nick. He wanted another two hundred a week. Said he had to have it. He laughed at me. There was a piece of pipe in the alley—"

After Tom had been taken away, Stan told Mary Adams. She sat in numb apathy until the shock dissolved itself into tears, accompanied by sobs that shook her heavily. He went over to her and after a while her sobs were less violent, and she took his hand and held it tightly.

HEADQUARTERS

(Continued from page 10)

one, friends—just the merest peek under the curtain. You've liked Kip Morgan before, so we're sure you're going to like him once again!

A Nick Ransom Novelet

More good news! Also in the next issue—SERENADE WITH SLUGS, by Robert Leslie Bellem. And—you're quite right in your surmise. He's back, all right! Two-fisted, wise-cracking, quick-thinking and ever genial ex-Hollywood stunt man—Nick Ransom—in person!

You'd never guess the place where Nick finds the body. Of all places for one to be—the Decker-Pasadena Funeral Home! It's no rib, folks. That's what Nick thought when he first went there. He asked the blond cutie receptionist—that's right—the one who wore the angora sweater—for Mr. Needham. Nick further embarrassed her by saying that Mr. Needham sent for him. Seeing how flustered the blond doll becomes, Nick asked.

"You mean Mr. Needham is a stiff?"

The situation is relieved by the arrival of Mr. Decker, slick and suave proprietor of

[*Turn page*]

the funeral parlors. It is true enough that Mr. Needham is dead and that even now, his body is being prepared. It is also true that Mr. Needham has sent for the "great detective." You see it is Mr. Paul Needham who is dead, but it is his brother Max who has sent for Ransom.

No Publicity Wanted

Mr. Decker goes on to explain that Mr. Max Needham doesn't want any publicity. Naturally Ransom knows who the brothers are—their address is in an exclusive yet slightly rundown neighborhood. They are worth millions, perhaps—yet they have lived practically as hermits for many, many years.

Suddenly, from behind the closed door of the room Nick Ransom is about to enter, comes the unmistakable sound of a shot. With the aid of his shoulder, Nick forces the door and enters the "repose" room. There is a corpse there right enough—but it is on the floor and not in a coffin where it should be. It is one of the Needham brothers too—but it is Max, and not Paul!

There is an open french door—the sound of footsteps, running along the gravel. Nick follows in quick pursuit of the sound, only to run into a blank, brick wall!

Solve this one, Nick Ransom! Of course you know he will, folks—but let us warn you, Nick will be at his busiest, his slam-bangest and his wisecrackingest, if we may coin a couple of words!

There will also be a swell selection of short stories by our usual lineup of sterling authors, next issue. As fine an issue as we have ever printed, and we realize that is going some!

OUR MAIL BOX

THE controversy of the quiet, suave and purely mental detective, versus the two-fisted, knock-down-and-drag-out dick, grows apace. We wish we had the time and the space to publish all of your letters, so we hope you'll all take this as a blanket series of thanks, bows and kudos to all of you kind people who have written in. Boiling it all down however, it seems as if, so far, the two-fisted boys are winning out.

Here's an interesting vote on the subject:

Hooray for all those biff-bang private eyes in THRILLING DETECTIVE Magazine. I've been a steady reader since your first Johnny Castle story. I refer, of course, to Race Williams and Nick Ransom. You can have these big, fat detectives who sit in padded armchairs, drink beer and *think* out the solutions of crimes. Give me the lads who *do* things, every time.—*Walter F. Burton, St. Louis, Mo.*

Thanks Walter! And here's another missive along the same lines:

My favorite magazine is THRILLING DETECTIVE. My favorite author is Robert Leslie Bellem and my favorite hero is Nick Ransom. When it comes to the girls, he certainly plays the field. So far, nobody has hooked him yet.—*Craig K. Ritchey, Chicago, Ill.*

You certainly have to give Nick credit, Craig. Glad you like him!

I like the magazine called THRILLING DETECTIVE because it has in it, stories by authors whose writings I enjoy a whole lot. I mean J. Lane Linklater, Edward Churchill, C. S. Montanye, Edward Ronns, Robert Leslie Bellem. Don't ever let us down.—*R. K. Westervelt, Prescott, Ariz.*

Thanks, pal. Now, the rest of you—keep those letters and post cards streaming in. Address them to the Editor, THRILLING DETECTIVE Magazine, 10 East 40th Street, New York 16, New York.

Again, thanks to all of you. See you next issue—and meanwhile happy reading to everybody!

—THE EDITOR.

The Fiction House Press Replica Line is available at www.FictionHousePress.com

Be sure to check our website regularly as we are constantly adding more pulp and digest replicas to our lineup.

www.ingramcontent.com/pod-product-compliance
Lightning Source LLC
LaVergne TN
LVHW061224100826
845148LV00004B/853